Jackpot.

By Ian Sears

1

The sun rises over the dark desert. A single beam races across the sand like a torpedo, heading straight for José's house. It sneaks in through a gap in the blinds and pokes him in the eye. He groans and sits up in his chair, rubs his face, straightens his greasy mustache. His blurry eyes focus on the kitchen table covered in cigarette butts and other people's poetry. What is he still looking for in these worn out books with their cracked spines and dead authors? A cure for his pain? A reason to return to life? He doesn't know anymore, doesn't care. He wipes his drool off the pages and picks up where he left off.

This isn't what his mama would have wanted. She'd always hoped he would go to America and make it big, and he would say no, Mama, those Americanos are too mean, all they care about is money! Mexico still has poets, I'll go find them and we'll all write for peace and justice, and she would shake her head and say José, you have no idea about Mexico, about the dark side of poetry. Don't repeat the past, don't be like your papa, please, go to America, get a job, stop wasting your time on books and cigarettes, I'm not made of money, you can't live here forever.

But then she died, and José inherited all she had. Alone in the world, his mama, papa, even his brother Jorge passed over to the other side, José was free at last to drift aimlessly through the days, melting into the silence of the desert until even the words in his books no longer made sounds in his mind. Mexico was for mañana until Mexico was forgotten, and the years dripped by like water through a canyon, carving out all else that might have been.

There's a knock at the door and he falls out of his chair. Shaking with terror, he gets his mama's revolver from the drawer. He takes a deep breath, then turns the knob and squints in the light. There's a gringo in a suit standing outside, his glossy black luxury vehicle parked by the mailbox.

"José Gonzales?"

José clears his throat and remembers how to speak. "Si."

"I represent the bank. I'm afraid your account with us has been running on empty for quite some time, and per our agreement we have no choice but to repossess some collateral."

"Collateral?"

"Yes, we've sent you a number of warnings. Are you not aware of the situation?"

José glances down at the pile of unopened mail on the floor. "No."

"Well, I hate to be the bearer of bad news, but the good news is it's simple. This house, the land it's sitting on, the assessed value of all your belongings—worthless. Almost, anyways. That's why we've got to nip this in the bud before your debts outweigh the value of your assets."

"My debts?"

"Here." The man from the bank hands him an envelope. "All pertinent details are enclosed. The bank has generously offered you a twenty-four hour window with which to make good on your outstanding balance, or we will be forced to evict you."

"No... this is my house!"

"I feel for you, sir, I really do. Fortunately, you have twenty four hours with which—"

"But I don't have any more money!"

"Well, maybe you can ask your parents, or a friend, or… someone."

José just stares at the ground.

"Well, I better get going. Lotta houses to hit. Have a nice day!" The man from the bank gets back in his glossy black luxury vehicle and kicks up a cloud of dust as he drives off.

José goes back inside and tries to read the letter, but his eyes glaze over at the long list of debts to be paid. He groans and throws it in the trash, runs his hands through his greasy black hair. He got the gist of it—he's fucked.

After an hour spent curled up in a ball sobbing on the kitchen floor, José dries his eyes, blows his nose, and looks around the home he's about to lose, at the business books his mama bought him and he never read, the posters on the wall of movies he's never seen, the family crucifix passed down through generations, his papa's signed portrait of a revolutionary whose revolution betrayed him. None of these dead objects answer his question: What's next? His head tells him Mexico. Go to the cafés, find the poets, return to life. But his heart tells him Honor Mama's wishes, go to America, make it big. So he packs his bag, tucks his gun in his pants, finds a few last coins in the drawer of his mama's nightstand, and gets in his papa's old pickup truck. He turns the keys and to his amazement the engine sputters to life. He takes one last look at the house he grew up in, the place that became his whole world—and drives away.

2

Having neglected to bring any water with him, José finds himself in desperate need of a drink. His mouth dry, his head pounding, he finally spots a lonesome shack in the distance, BAR painted on the roof in red letters.

He pulls up in the dirt lot and parks his rusty pickup.

His spurs rattle when his boots hit the dust.

All heads turn as the double doors swing open. José squints and sizes 'em all up, then saunters up to the bartender and puts a coin down.

"One drink, please."

The bartender pours him a tall one and slides it over.

"Ain't seen you round these parts."

"I'm a roamer," says José. "I do my thing out here, wandering the desert, and I don't abide by any rules." He toasts to the sky and his glass sparkles. "Dios guía mi corazón!"

The bartender frowns.

"Look, hombre, I don't care which rules you don't abide by so long as you abide by that one!" He points to a sign above the liquor that says "Talk American!"

"Porque? You don't like Spanish?"

"Nope. Can't speak it, won't learn it. If you don't like it, you can leave."

José's about to retort when a trio of mustachioed bandits burst through the doors. They fire their revolvers in the air and the bullets punch holes in the ceiling and kill the TV. Sparks spill out the busted screen and set some clothes on fire and the people inside them yelp and knock over chairs and pour drinks on each other.

"Nobody move!" shouts the leader. "Even if you're on fire! Come on, stop squirming around! This is a stickup, there are rules—"

In three swift shots, José shoots the bandits dead. The bar is silent, save the crackling death rattle of the shattered television. Everyone realizes it ain't a stickup no more and they put their hands down, extinguish the fires, and get back to drinking. José takes a swig.

"So what was it you were saying about talking American?" he says in such a way that, if you knew Spanish, you'd want to run straight out of there and call your mama.

"Nada, señor, nada!"

The bartender flips the "Talk American" sign around and starts re-organizing some bottles.

"Correctamundo." José chugs the rest of his drink and slams the empty glass down on the bar.

"One more drink, comin' right up!" The bartender pours another and slides it down the bar, but José misses the catch and spills it all over himself. Everyone laughs and his confidence vanishes. He doesn't understand. He just killed some outlaws! He's supposed to be a hero!

"Stop it! Por favor! Don't be mean to me! Please!" But his protests only fuel their mockery. In a last ditch effort to preserve his dignity, José straightens up and lays his American on thick. "Guess I better mosey on out for a spell to dry off."

The laughter only grows louder. Nobody's buying the tough guy act after all that whimpering, the bartender even flips the "Talk American" sign back around. Struggling to keep the pain inside, José soldiers past the other patrons, carefully stepping over the bodies of the mustachioed bandits as he goes back out into the merciful heat.

He takes off his wet shirt and lays it flat on the hood of his pickup. When he's sure nobody's looking, he lets a single tear streak naked down his cheek. How could he have been such a fool? If only he'd caught the drink, if only he'd stayed tough the whole time, if only—let it go, José. What's done is done. Dazed by the heat and drink and his turbulent emotions, he wishes he had a cigarette to straighten him out, then roots around in his pockets and finds an old grape lollipop. He unwraps it, pops it in his mouth, and instinctively pulls out a lighter. Just as the flame licks the stick, he remembers a promise he made to his mama, a promise to quit smoking. He sighs and puts the lighter back in his pocket.

"No way, José. Not today."

The bartender and a couple patrons come out dragging the mustachioed bandits. Eager to repair his image, José tries to lean against his truck like a cool guy, but it burns his skin and he cries out in pain and drops the lollipop. The undertakers glance over, but luckily they're too busy to make fun of him. The bodies paint thick red stripes in the sand.

An engine sounds in the distance. Ahoy! A great white van appears over yonder, rumbling through the desert. José pulls out his binoculars. There's a hissing rattlesnake wrapped around a television painted on the side and the text below reads: "Rattlesnake Television Repair: Don't Tread on Us!" Soon the van pulls up to the bar and a tall cowboy carrying a toolbox steps out. His warm eyes have seen the worst in men, and he gives José a toothy grin.

"I heard some banditos broke your TV."

José lowers his binoculars. "You heard right."

"Reckon I could take a look?"

"Sure. The owner's out back, but he'll be around in a second."

"Then I guess for now I'll take a look from out here. You mind?"

José hands the cowboy his binoculars. He peers through the window and whistles.

"Now that's a doozy. I'll see what I can do. Thanks, partner." He hands them back.

The undertakers come back round front, their hands covered in blood.

"Well if it ain't Leroy McMenahan!" says the bartender.

"Howdy."

The bartender looks at his hands and chuckles. "Apologies for my appearance. There were some—"

"No need to explain. Bandit troubles, I take it?"

"Yes, sir, but we took care of 'em just fine."

"You mean I took care of them," says José.

Leroy furrows his brow. "Is that so?"

The bartender's smile goes flat. "Yes, sir."

"I see. Well how about y'all go clean up while me and, what'd you say your name was?"

"José."

"While me and José fix that television set. You wouldn't mind giving me a hand, would you?"

"Not at all," says José, grinning wide. This is just what he needed. If he can share some of the credit for getting the TV fixed, everyone will have no choice but to respect him again! Leroy holds the door open for the undertakers so they don't get blood on it. José slips his shirt back on, puffs out his chest, and follows them inside.

The TV's still sparking and belching smoke and the hole in the screen is only getting wider as shards of glass break off and shatter on the floor.

"I was right about this one being a doozy," says Leroy. "But it ain't nothing we can't fix! Why don't you sweep up the glass while I find the right tools?" He opens up his toolbox and José grabs a broom and dustpan. He sweeps like a maniac, inspired by Leroy's optimism in the face of the most horrific television mutilation he's ever seen. Soon enough, the bar's kind of clean and Leroy's ready for action. He shoves the tangle of wires back into the screen and stretches out a swath of tape. José wipes a bucket's worth of sweat off his brow and tries to keep his teeth from chattering. Leroy's only got one shot at this, and if it doesn't go right—well, José doesn't want to think about that.

The tape makes contact. Leroy slowly guides it along the glass and over the hole. José can't bear to watch but he can't look away. A few swaths later, Leroy seals the patch and turns the TV on. A blizzard of static fills the screen and slowly clears up until some yankee reading the news comes into focus.

"Good as new," says Leroy, wiping nothing off his hands.

Everyone in the bar cheers and gives them a round of applause.

"Now how about some drinks?"

"Two drinks, comin' right up!" The bartender pours 'em up and slides 'em over. Neither spill.

Leroy raises his glass. "To a job well done!"

José raises his and they clink and drink up. As the ice cold drink takes the edge off for Leroy, he notices José is still wound up tight.

"What's wrong, buddy?"

"Nada, nothing." José takes another sip.

Leroy looks around and spots the "Talk American" sign. "Were they—were they being prejudiced towards you before I showed up?"

José takes another sip. Leroy catches the bartender's eye and the bartender looks away and starts a conversation

10

about the weather with a patron in the corner, passed out drunk. Leroy shakes his head and climbs up onto the bar.

"Listen up, y'all!"

All heads turn, except some gamblers in the corner watching the horse race.

"Y'all better turn that TV off before I break it again."

The gamblers ignore him but the bartender rushes over and switches it off.

"It has come to my attention that racial prejudice, no longer the law of the land, no longer socially acceptable, never right in the first place, is still welcome in this establishment. Am I wrong?"

Besides some muted grumbling, nobody says anything.

"I said, am I wrong?"

The patrons shake their heads in shame.

"Come on now, y'all, that ain't how we do things no more! We won World War II out in Europe and the Pacific, but it seems to me we ain't done winning it here at home. In our hearts." He taps his heart a couple times. "Now I don't care who did it or who didn't, I want every last one of y'all to apologize to José. We can get it over with quick. Ready? One, two, three."

"Sorry, José," says everyone. Everyone but the bartender.

Leroy walks down the bar and crouches to look him in the eye. "We got a problem?"

"I ain't saying sorry if I ain't sorry."

"I reckon you'd better, old buddy, or you're about to be."

The bartender frowns, but he knows Leroy don't make idle threats. He turns to José. "I'm sorry."

"Come on now, say it with a little more feeling."

"It's okay, Leroy," says José. "Apology accepted."

The bartender snorts, then disappears into the bathroom.

Leroy hops down and reclaims his seat. "There now, that better?"

José smiles. "Si." Actually, he's pretty embarrassed, and he knows most of those apologies were baloney. But it's nice to have a guy like Leroy stick up for him.

They clink glasses and take another drink.

"Now don't you worry about folks with prejudice no more, you hear me? They're just a pack of fools. This is America, you work hard and you make your way and you get what you get!"

"Okay."

"There you go! Let me tell you, I wasn't always a television repairman. No sir, I worked my way up from nothing and here I am. You see..." Soon the heroic duo are deep in conversation, blazing through their drinks on autopilot, having a damn good time. Caught up in the heat of the moment, they swipe a sombrero from a sun-dried old vaquero who'd just wanted to enjoy his day off. They head out back and play monkey in the middle with it. The vaquero keeps tripping over the bandits' corpses as he runs back and forth.

"Come on, old timer, is that the best you can do?" shouts Leroy.

"Si," he wheezes. "Please, give it back. My mama made it for me many years ago. She died when I was young, and it's the only thing I have left to remember her by."

"Sure, you can have it back," says Leroy, throwing it.

"When you catch it!" shouts José, catching it with glee.

The vaquero trips over a bandit and accidentally kisses another one on the lips.

"Gross!" says José.

The three amigos share a laugh, even the vaquero once he's done spluttering.

"Alright, you old fossil, we'll give you one more chance to catch it!" José reaches all the way back and tosses the sombrero as hard as he can. The vaquero springs into action, but the hat sails over his head and far past Leroy, gliding through the desert air with the grace of a UFO over Area 51.

"No!" The vaquero watches helplessly as the sombrero lands on the main trunk of a tall saguaro cactus. From afar, the cactus now looks like a friendly renegade, arms stretched upwards, ready to give a prickly hug to whoever wants one. As the vaquero sprints towards it, cursing our heroes in vulgar Spanish, the sun begins to set. José and Leroy glance over at each other, their minds tuned to the same thought:

Jackpot.

3

José's broke but Leroy's got some dough saved up. The deal is, Leroy makes his money back first, then they split it fifty-fifty. But before that can happen, they need to find some kind of economy, a real one, not like round these parts, so they drop Leroy's van off at the shop and drive deeper into the desert.

The road ends at the grandest canyon of them all, The Grand Canyon. They roll right up to the edge and get out.

"Damn it!" Leroy throws his hat on the ground and his voice echoes across the open miles. "This'll take forever to get around!"

José stands at the rim, contemplating the majesty of nature.

"Well," says Leroy, "I reckon we can stop in town for the night. Make our way round tomorrow." He walks back to the truck.

José pulls out his gun, looks at it for a moment, then tosses it over the edge. Shots ring out as it bounces down the rocks.

"What the hell'd you do that for?!" shouts Leroy, covering his ears.

"I don't want to use it ever again!"

Leroy's pissed. He thinks José's being naive, but there's no denying the nobility of his gesture. He holds his tongue, gets in the truck, and waits until José's ready. When he climbs into the passenger seat, no words pass between them. Leroy starts the engine and they head around another way, following signs for a nearby town.

A couple miles out they spot a ragged old man shuffling along the side of the road. Leroy pumps the brakes and José rolls down his window.

"Need a ride?"

"Where you headed?"

"Going into town," says Leroy.

The old man shakes his head like an electric toothbrush. "No thanks! Anywhere but that hellhole!"

"What's wrong with it?" asks José.

"You wouldn't believe me if I told you."

"Oh yeah?"

"Yeah. So forget it!"

José shrugs. "Alright, geezer."

The old man is offended. He's no geezer, it's just the booze!

"By the way, where's a good place to stay around here?" asks José.

The old man thinks about it and decides to repay José's insult. "Well, there's the inn, but that's mighty expensive. I lived above my gift shop on Main Street, but I don't reckon I'm ever going back. Here." He tosses José a ring of keys. "It's yours now." The old man chuckles and resumes his trek.

"I guess there is such thing as a free lunch!"

"Maybe," says Leroy, but something don't feel right.

It's dusk when they roll into town. Main Street is deserted. There's a thin dirt lot behind the gift shop, and that's where they park the pickup. The faded sign above the door reads: Desert Knick Knacks and Grand Souvenirs. The shop is dark and dusty. José fumbles for the lights and eventually turns them on. Seems the old man left in a hurry. There's still money in the register, the sign in the front window is still flipped to "OPEN," and the bent ceiling fan is still spinning on its lopsided axis. Mystery is in the air. Upstairs there's a small kitchen and two bedrooms. Why that lonely old man would need two bedrooms is beyond Leroy, but José senses the absence of a child. Clothes are strewn across the old man's bed. A suitcase lies half-packed on the floor.

"Wonder why he was in such a hurry?" says Leroy.

"Maybe he had some trouble with the law."

"Could be."

But no officers come knocking, and José and Leroy turn in for the night. The full moon shines bright and coyotes howl in the distance. Leroy's fast asleep, but something's bothering José. He stares up at the ceiling, his dry eyes unable to stay shut, his ears tuned in to every little sound. He wonders why the old man's TV has a bright red light next to its power button to show that it's off. He can see damn well that it's off, because it's not on. He gets up and unplugs it. Footsteps. Cold sweat drenches his nightcap. Something gets knocked over down in the store. He tiptoes across the kitchen and down the stairs, wishing he hadn't thrown his gun off a cliff. All he has now are his trusty fists, Rupert and Percy, names that once sounded tough and romantic, but now strike him as wimpy and bourgeois. Percy flips on the lights. The store is empty, but the back door is swinging open and shut in the breeze. The stand of novelty license plates rolls back and forth across the floor, half its plates scattered.

"Just the wind," says José, chuckling. He shuts the door, rights the stand, and goes back to sleep.

In the morning Leroy cooks up some eggs, double-over western jackalope-style with a little pepper, just the way he likes 'em.

"Think we can make it to California today?" José asks between mouthfuls.

16

"Maybe. But I've been thinking. Why not set up shop here? The old man gave us the place, and half the trouble in business is getting a store!"

José mulls it over.

"And," Leroy adds, "we're right next to the grandest tourist attraction in the whole U.S. of A!"

"You know what," says José, pointing his fork, "you've got a point."

"We'll spend our principal setting up ties with a factory that can—"

Outside, someone screams. Our heroic duo run down through the gift shop and out the door to find some townsfolk gathered around. Someone's scrawled "LEAVE" in red on the front windows, and there's a dead chicken lying in a pool of blood on the sidewalk.

"What the hell?" asks Leroy.

"Who are you?" asks a burly young man who could have been a great quarterback if only he'd listened to his coach and given it a hundred and ten percent during practice and gametime, no matter what.

"We're the new proprietors of Desert Knick Knacks and Grand Souvenirs," says Leroy, reading off the sign. "Ran into the old owner out on the road and he gave us the keys. Didn't want nothing to do with it no more."

"I don't blame him. Place has been haunted ever since he inherited it from my father."

The crowd begins to disperse.

"Haunted?" asks Leroy.

"Your father?" asks José.

"Yes, sir," he says, grinning. "The name's James Calahan."

"Leroy McMenahan."

"José... Jones."

"Pleasure."

They shake hands.

"As I was saying, when my father died, he left the shop to Frank Rodenbelt, no relation mind you. Anyways, him and old Frank went way back, friends since they were kids. Me, I would have been just fine running the store myself, but my father wouldn't hear of it. He wanted me to go to college to study hydro engineering, but here I am now with a piece of paper and no dams to my name."

"I see," says Leroy. "How long's this haunting been going on?"

"Quite some time now, I'm afraid. About a week after I got back to town, Frank started telling people he was seeing ghosts and hearing voices telling him to clear out."

"Really?" asks José, pale as a ghost himself.

"Yes, sir. I took a look for myself a few times, but I never saw anything unusual until this."

José crosses himself.

"Well, I reckon we'd better clean up all this blood," says Leroy.

"Wait a second," says James. "I understand old Frank said you could have this place, but he was in no condition to be making such an important decision. Now, seeing as this was my father's store and all, I think it would only be fair if—"

Leroy holds up his hand. "We're keeping the store."

"But—"

"I won't hear it. Frank gave us this store for a reason, I feel it in my bones. I refuse to go against his wishes."

James is furious but holds back. "Fine. Just don't come crying to me if you see any... *ghosts*!" He walks away, cackling.

"Oh, Leroy, I sure hope he's fibbing about those ghosts!" says José, shivering.

"I wouldn't worry about it. I ain't one to believe in such things. Only notions of facts and science floatin' round in this head," says Leroy, tapping his head. He goes inside and finds a mop and bucket. The window is dyed pink as the blood washes down, but looks clean as ever after a second washing. Leroy picks the chicken up by its feet and throws it in the trash, and José breathes a sigh of relief as the bloody water trickles into the gutter.

"Just one thing I can't put my finger on," says Leroy. "Who, or what, would write such a thing on our store?"

José thinks. "El Chupacabra?"

"Could be... but why?" They go back inside and a crow caws.

Despite all their unanswered questions, they're able to put the incident out of their minds and get to work. They spend the rest of the day planning, contacting potential manufacturers, and selling knick knacks to the occasional tourist. The sun sinks into the canyon and they get ready for bed.

Leroy shuts his eyes and pulls the covers up high, ready for a good night's sleep after a long day. Right as he's about to drift off, he hears a scream. He jolts up. Did he imagine it? No, because he hears it again. It's José. Leroy jumps out of bed and into his slippers. He runs through the kitchen and tries the door to José's room. It's locked. The screams get louder. He kicks his way in and sees a ghost standing on the end of José's bed, flapping around.

"Woooooo!" the ghost shouts. "I'm a ghost! Leave this place at once! Woooooo!"

José can't stop screaming and pulls his sheets up to his mouth. Leroy flips on the light. The ghost, really just someone wearing a large bed sheet, jumps off the bed and tries to climb out the window, but Leroy grabs him by the foot and pulls him back inside.

"Don't hurt me!" the ghost whimpers, clawing at the rug. Leroy reaches down and pulls the sheet off.

"James Calahan?!" Leroy and José exclaim in unison.

"Dang nabbit! You got me."

"Why'd you do it, James?" José asks from his bed.

James doesn't respond.

"I think I can explain," says Leroy, holding up a finger. "It all started when his father died. Young James here had been expecting to inherit the store, but in a twist of fate, it went to Frank Rodenbelt. Rather than accepting the wishes of his father, James devised an ingenious plan to spook old Frank into turning it over to him: he'd dress up as a ghost and haunt the place until Frank couldn't take it no more. Except he spooked old Frank a little too much, you see, and we got the store instead. Now—" Leroy's explanation is cut off by a roaring wind. Papers and books circle the room and the three men cower in terror as a towering, bearded specter appears before them.

"Enough!" booms the specter.

"Dad?" asks James, peering out from under the bed.

"Yes, it is I, Robert Calahan, your father!" The specter strokes his majestic beard. "Why haven't you built any dams, my son?"

"Why didn't you give me the store?"

"Why the hell would I give you the store? You always hated this place, making you work here after school was like waging war! I want no more excuses! I didn't shell out five hundred dollars for that prophecy so you could sit on your ass selling knick knacks! Do what the mystic Sara said, journey to the dry city of Los Angeles. There you shall find great demand for dam builders."

"Dad, I told you, I don't care about that stupid prophecy. I'm just trying to make some money and live my life."

"Then why'd you go through four years of hydro engineering school?"

"Because you made me!"

"Hah! You were eighteen, boy, I didn't make you do anything! Talk about making money—you'd make ten times as much building dams and you know it! Look at your life, my son. You're dressing up as a ghost and scaring people, but you're the one who's scared."

"Scared of what?"

"Of growing up!" shouts José, tears in his eyes. "Your dad loves you, he's trying to set you up with a good life! Don't you see that?" He hides under the covers and sobs.

The specter scratches his head. "Did Frank really give it to you two?"

"Yes, sir," says Leroy.

"Then it is yours."

José and Leroy yeehaw.

"But Dad—"

The specter places a ghostly hand on James' shoulder. "My son, your destiny lies not in this store, but in the great waterless lands to the west! The climate's a'changing, my boy! Go forth, and through hard work and perseverance, you shall discover the true meaning of..." The specter rambles on for another twenty minutes. Comfortable in his bed, José falls back asleep. Leroy barely manages to stay awake, resorting to pinching and even slapping himself. James is also bored by his father's speech, but since it's directed at him he's forced to work eleven times as hard to pay attention. A sigh of relief is shared amongst the living as the specter's speech ends.

"'...Do not go gentle into that good night. Rage, rage against the dying of the light.' And with that, I bid you farewell. Until we meet again." The ferocious wind returns to the room, blowing in the opposite direction as last time.

The scattered papers and books find their way back to their original places. The specter has vanished. James wipes a tear from his eye.

"He always was a windbag. Ain't nothing death can change about that."

Leroy looks over at José, fast asleep. "You want to finish this in the kitchen?"

"I was thinking the same thing."

James and Leroy tiptoe out of there.

"Well, I reckon I better head on down to Los Angeles."

"Agreed."

"I'm sorry about trying to haunt you and all. That was mighty foolish of me."

"Don't mention it, kid. Everyone makes mistakes."

"Thank you, sir."

"Now get the heck out of here and make your dad proud!"

"Yes, sir!" James Calahan dashes off, forgetting his sheet, forgetting the store, forgetting everything except the dusty road to the city of angels.

A month goes by. José and Leroy have replaced all the old knick knacks with their own merchandise, but business is slow. How could these foolish tourists fail to appreciate the genius of the saguaro sombrero pennants, mugs, ashtrays, placemats, action figures, plush dolls, paintings, bumper stickers, temporary tattoos, and of course, the actual cacti wearing sombreros tactically positioned throughout the store, cacti that José and Leroy spent a whole day out in the desert digging up and dodging park rangers to retrieve?

A tan old lady wearing all sorts of crystal jewelry walks in, looks around, and leaves without buying anything. José slams his fist down on the counter and holds back tears.

"What are we doing wrong?"

"I don't know, José. If I did, I'd sure as hell tell you. Be patient, alright?"

José blows his nose and wipes his eyes. "I know, I know. It just feels like something's missing."

Leroy strokes his stubble, deep in thought. He remains frozen in place for the rest of the day. Seeing a chance to save a couple bucks, José takes the batteries out of the clock and uses Leroy as a sundial. When the sun hangs low and shines into Leroy's squinting eyes, José draws the blinds and locks up for the night.

"Come on Leroy, let's go get a bite to eat."

Leroy nods but José doubts he really heard him. Once Leroy gets those thinking gears turning, there ain't no stopping them.

They arrive at a blossoming Mexican restaurant. Blossoming because it's new, the only new place in town, always adding new things, new specials, new paintings, new ferns, new fish in the aquarium, potted flowers in every corner, on every table, flowers on the wallpaper, flowers in the funny cigarettes the dishwashers smoke out back. Forty-five years later, at the height of Sino-American tensions, it receives a one-star review on the internet and goes out of business. But for now, it's a fine establishment that serves good food to good people.

The waiter directs José and Leroy to their usual table in the corner. A five-piece mariachi band walks between tables performing a beautiful, heart-wrenching rendition of "La Cucaracha." José weeps as he shovels fistfulls of tortilla chips into his mouth. Leroy gazes at the band, not so much listening as admiring the dexterity of each musician. The singer breaks into a spicy maracas solo and time slows to a crawl. Leroy can hear every ball sliding around inside those waving red shells, each micro-collision carefully controlled by the singer's deft wrists. The gears finish turning.

"I've got it!"

"What?" José sobs.

"Our idea... you were right, José, it was only half finished! Putting a sombrero on a cactus was pure genius, but if we have it hold maracas too, there's no way we can lose!"

José spits his chips out all over the table. "Leroy, that's perfect! It's gonna change everything!"

The waiter returns. "Are you gentlemen ready to order?"

Leroy drains his water and crunches down on an ice cube. "I think we'll take this meal to go."

4

One year later, José and Leroy have an office in Los Angeles overlooking the beach. They each have their own apartment nearby and are living the high life. The name of their company, Saguaro Sombrero Solutions Unlimited, is not well known to those outside the business world. But their products are. These days, you'd be hard-pressed to find anyone unfamiliar with the image of a smiling cactus wearing a sombrero and shaking some maracas. From Mexican restaurants to tacky gift shops, from children's television to high-class tequila labels, the sombrero-clad saguaro is ever-present in modern life. And it's all thanks to the vision of José Jones and Leroy McMenahan.

José and Leroy are currently hosting an Important Client in their corner office. A deal has been struck, and the three titans of industry light cigarillos in celebration.

"I'm glad you gentlemen were able to see things my way. With this new logo, our product is poised to corner an entirely untapped section of the market." The Important Client's fat, balding head glistens in the sunlight as he puffs away at his cigarillo beneath his greasy moustache.

"It wouldn't be half the logo without those maracas," José says. "Those were Leroy's idea."

The Important Client gives José a phony smile. José clenches his cigarillo in his teeth and smiles back, but in his heart a sad flamenco tune plays as he realizes that by smoking, even for business, he has once again broken the promise he made to his mama. Without thinking, out of pure reflex, he composes an earth-shakingly beautiful quintilla and nearly weeps when he realizes there isn't a soul in the world capable of comprehending the depth of his sorrow.

"Mama," he whispers, taking another puff despite his shame. "Forgive me."

"You alright, José?" asks Leroy.

José bursts into a fit of coughing. "Si, si, I'm fine. Excuse me." Still coughing, he dashes off to the bathroom.

"My apologies, sir. José just hasn't been himself lately. Must be coming down with something."

The Important Client squints, disapproving of Leroy's explanation. "I see." He takes a long drag from his cigarillo, then blows smoke at a bonsai tree on José's desk. It withers and dies. "Let me tell you something, McMenahan. In this world, there are two types of people. Those with vision, and those who seek to profit from the sweat of another man's brow. There are Creators, and there are parasites. Now it's plain to see that you're a Creator. You were the one who came up with the maracas idea, you were the one who banished James Calahan from his father's gift shop, and most Importantly, you were the one who approached Me."

"José was an equal part of—"

"Don't sell yourself short, McMenahan! Yes, José may have been there for those endeavors but they were *your* endeavors. Now I am not suggesting outright that José is leeching off the hard-earned fruits of your labor, but a man who leaves a meeting with a Client as Important as Me? All because he can't smoke a cigarillo like a man? That is not behavior I ascribe to Creators." He drapes a fat, heavy arm over Leroy's shoulder. "What I'm saying is you've got talent. Business talent." He hands Leroy his personal business card. "Perhaps you and I can conduct some business of our own."

"Sir, you are gravely mistaken if you're suggesting that José is some sort of burden. I would never—"

The Important Client holds up his hand. "Sleep on it."

Leroy's about to retort when José slinks back into the room.

"Well, I'd best be on my way. An Important Client such as Myself has lots of Important Business to attend to." He shakes Leroy's hand, crushes José's, and glides out of the room. José and Leroy are silent as the Important Client makes his way to the elevator and presses down. The doors open and he steps inside. He turns to face them and smiles.

"One of you will go on to great things." He bursts into laughter as the doors close and the co-CEOs hear it echo up the shaft. They go to the window. A chauffeur holds open the door of a pitch black limo. The Important Client looks up at them and winks before getting in.

"Are you alright?" Leroy asks as the limo drives off.

"Si, I'm sorry about that."

Michael Sweeney, a ladder-climbing go-getter hired by Leroy to get things done, runs into the room.

"Did the deal go through?"

"Sure did, Micky," says Leroy, grinning wide. José spots his wilted bonsai tree and gasps, and Leroy is filled with the melancholy of a compassionate cowboy victorious after a gunfight. "But it cost us."

Michael's shocked. Leroy's never lost money on a deal!

"How much?"

José cradles his dead tree in his arms, praying to God that his tears might water it back to life. "We lost something money can't buy! I'm sorry—" He runs out of the office.

"You know, they're selling bonsais down at—"

"It's not about the damn tree, Micky!" Leroy shouts, slamming his fist down on the desk. The heads of every office drone snap up, then sink back down to their work. "I'm sorry, kid. You're trying your best."

"I am."

"Don't get cocky now."

"Yes, sir." Michael spins around and gets back to work.

Leroy stubs his still-burning cigarillo in the ashtray and leans back in his chair, wondering what dark presence José saw in the deal, or the Important Client, or the death of his bonsai. Something slick and cold fills his empty stomach.

By the next quarter, it's clear the deal has been a huge success. Leroy buys a new car, Michael gets promoted, and Saguaro Sombrero Solutions Unlimited opens a new factory over by the airplane graveyard. José, of course, buys himself a new bonsai. He pours his heart into his new tree, spending hours watering and preening it, adjusting its spot in the office as the light changes throughout the day.

Yet despite the joy his new tree has brought him, there remains a quiet sadness behind every clip of his shears, every drop of water he pours, every gentle caress of the tree's tender branches.

Soon everyone can tell that José's spending more time on the tree than on work. Dissatisfaction and rumors spread among the drones like a flask and a bad cold through a band of hobos. Michael, go-getter that he is, sees an opportunity. He tightens his tie, blows his nose, and hopes no one can tell he's drenched in sweat. He knocks on the door of the corner office. Leroy lets him in.

The office has changed a lot since the big deal, José's half anyways. A web of caution tape surrounds his immaculate bonsai tree. Watering cans litter the floor. No

28

smoking signs are nailed to his desk and the walls. Light green moss inches across the carpet towards Leroy's side, stopped only by a wall of metal rulers glued end to end, dividing the room in two. José could be hidden somewhere in the clutter and Michael would never know.

"Have a seat," Leroy tells him.

Michael sits. "Is José in?"

"Nope. That's why you're here, right? To tell me everyone's had it with his whole—this?" he says, gesturing at José's jungle.

Michael gulps. "Yes, sir. You see, we all know this company wouldn't be here without José, it's just…" Michael trails off as Leroy cracks a window and takes a contemplative drag of his hand-rolled cigarillo. He breathes out through his nose and mouth and the smoke takes the form of a cactus.

"Say no more. I reckon this day's been coming a while now."

"You do?"

Leroy nods and sucks air through his teeth. "Me and José go way back. I can always sense these things."

"Wow."

"Yeah. Now if you'll excuse me, I need some time to think."

"Yes, sir!" Michael walks out with some zip in his step. When the door closes behind him, he rubs his hands together and chuckles ominously.

When José gets back from the store, Leroy waits for him to put his stuff down, then asks him to come over to his desk. José takes a seat.

"Do you remember the day you got your first bonsai?"

José nods, then pulls out a tissue and fails to close the floodgates. God, this is already going terrible. Leroy shifts in his seat and scans his desk, desperate for a distraction. He picks up a half-finished sudoku, and by the time he finishes, José has pretty much pulled himself together. Leroy continues.

"Well I don't know exactly what happened that day, but something changed you. Or it changed the way you feel about what we're doing here. Am I right?"

José sniffs. "Si."

"Do you think you can explain it to me?"

"No."

"That's what I thought." Leroy sighs. "José, do you really want to keep working here?"

José is silent for a moment. "I don't think so. I think I'll go mad if I stay here. Perhaps I already have." He laughs and gestures at his jungle.

Leroy doesn't say anything but his eyes tell José that he's seen his share of madness, and he doesn't quite fit the bill. Not yet, anyhow.

"We'll work something out with the lawyers—"

"I trust you, Leroy."

Now it's Leroy's turn to shed a tear.

José knows he's leaving the only friend he's got, but he shakes Leroy's hand, picks up his bonsai, and walks through the office. When he reaches the elevator, he turns to look at everyone for the last time and they forget all the gossip and rumors and stand in unison to salute the departure of a true business visionary.

5

José broods through the dust and trash along crumbling sidewalks. The half-dead buildings with their faded signs and dirty windows look slanted and menacing, as if they might fall on him at any moment in revenge against the neighborhood. He trashes his company badge and jolts when a sombrero-clad saguaro inked onto an empty tequila bottle smiles up at him, cheerfully waving its maracas. He takes a deep breath and squints his way across the blinding concrete. He could really use some sunglasses. At the end of the block he spots a Sun Shack and peers through the window. Look at all those happy people, trying on aviators and wayfarers and God knows what else. It makes him sick. Don't they know buying a pair of sunglasses won't solve their problems? He spits and it streaks down the window.

"Right on, man."

José turns around. There's a hipster wearing a beanie, cardigan, and jeans despite the heat, his eyes shaded with a pair of circles.

"Fuck the system, am I right?"

José's not sure about this guy. "Si."

"Spanish. Nice, man."

The customers are glaring at them, but the hipster doesn't seem to notice.

"You... like Spanish?" asks José.

"I like all languages, brother. I'm a poet!"

"Really?"

The hipster rolls his eyes. "No, I'm just messing with you. Come on, of course I'm a fucking poet! You like poetry?"

"Do I like it? Poetry is my life!"

"That's what's up, man! I could tell you were a real one. So check it, we've got an open mic at six over at the Imperial Roastery if you want to come listen. Maybe you could even read some of your own stuff. What do you say?"

Tears in his eyes, José trembles with gratitude. "I would be honored."

"Check, check. One, two, check. Check." The MC taps the mic and feedback pierces the coffeeshop.

José's sweating in a tuxedo in the back corner, awaiting his execution. He straightens his papers but his sweaty fingers smudge the ink and he panics and scatters them all over the table.

The hipster walks over carrying a battered notebook.

"Yo, you made it! Are you gonna read?"

José gulps and nods.

The hipster smirks. "It's alright to be nervous, man. Bearing your soul to the public is no easy task. They should give us medals." He extends a friendly hand. "I'm Pete, by the way."

José shakes his hand. "José."

Pete takes a seat and takes off his beanie. "Now tell me, José, what are you running from?"

"What am I running from?"

Pete runs his hand through his charged hair. "Yeah, man. We're all running from something, you know? That's why we're here. To stop running. Together." He puts both hands on José's shoulders and stares deep into his eyes.

"Tell me what happened. The vibes were low when I met you, bro—what was going on under the awn? Ing?"

José takes a deep breath, too focused on working up the courage to tell his story to recall whether the Sun Shack had an awning. "Well, I'd just quit my business. You see, my friend and I started a successful company, and at first things were great, but then—"

"But then things got too corporate, huh? All about the money and nothing about the passion, right?"

"Sure, maybe, but it's not just—"

"Well right on José. We're all running from corporate greed in our own ways. Just take a look outside. Society's fucked." He leans back and taps his head. "You want to know what I'm running from?"

"Okay."

"It's a story I'm sure you know quite well, but I'll tell it anyway." A crowd gathers around their table. "July sixteenth, nineteen oh seven. Brazil, Indiana. A baby boy is born, a boy who will one day grow into a man who will change the world—I think you know where this is going."

"No, I don't."

"Well you should, because that man's name was Argile Pepinpopper."

José scratches his head. "The popcorn guy?"

"More like the Popcorn Tycoon! Anyways, through entrepreneurship and ingenuity, he *popped* right out of his small-town beginnings—" Pete pauses to let the crowd laugh. "And into homes and theaters across America."

"What does this have to do with you?"

The crowd gasps.

Pete holds up a silencing hand. "Please, José, let me finish. Argile Pepinpopper had a son, and then his son had a son, you with me? That son, José, is my third cousin, and as long as I can remember, I've lived in the shadow of the

Pepinpopper name. It follows me everywhere, casting a buttery light on everything I do!"

Some bystanders wipe away tears.

José wrinkles his eyebrows, failing to understand how a shadow can cast a buttery light. "Pete."

"What?"

"If you're so worried about that name following you, maybe you should stop telling people about it."

Pete slams the table and peanut shells float up like reverse confetti. "Are you saying my pain is bullshit?"

"No, it's just if you let go of the past, maybe—"

The crowd boos.

Pete stands up. "You just crossed the wrong poet, hombre. I'll see you on stage." Pete snaps his fingers and his entourage follows him across the coffeeshop. The lights dim and the MC retakes the stage.

"Welcome, everyone," he says, his smooth voice melting the tension. "Welcome... to you. Tonight is not only about the people performing. It's about stories and passion. It's about sharing an experience. It's about... you."

The audience erupts in snapping. Pete shudders in agony, the cacophony reminding him of microwave popcorn.

"Please welcome our first reader, a woman we all know well, Jacintha Crothers!"

The crowd snaps up a storm and Jacintha takes the stage.

"Thanks everybody, thank you. You're too kind. Thank you. It means so much to be here, in front of you all, reading my poetry. It's so important to have a space like this where our voices can be heard."

"That's right!"

"Tell it!"

Jacintha smiles. "Without you, I'd just have to read to my cat, and what's the point of that? So thank you all. This means so much. You have no idea." She clears her throat and reads a poem called "Your Ears are Like Music to My Mouth," a long, free-verse testament to how much it means to her that other people listen to her read her poetry, a winding chronicle that takes up her entire slot. The audience snaps and cheers once more and Jacintha exits with a bow and a smile. Good for her, getting up there like that, thinks José, putting a positive spin on her set after his visceral, obsessive disagreement with her claim that there's no point in reading poetry to a cat.

One by one the readers walk on stage, read beyond their five minute time limit, and soak up the snaps. Pete slowly, but never completely, adjusts to the sound. A woman sitting near José says things like "uh-huh," "word," and "she *gets* it," throughout every poem, her admiration taking on its own poetic rhythm. José finds it very distracting. By the time Pete slithers up to the mic, she's ecstatic, and so is everyone else.

"Yeah, Pete!" she shouts. "Tell it like it *is*!"

Pete winks at her. He taps the microphone and it softly booms like distant fireworks. He feigns humble nervousness and motions for everyone to settle down.

"Thank you. And thanks to all the other communicators who've read tonight." A few bold cheers shoot out. Pete smiles and waits an extra second. "Thank you. I could introduce myself, but I'd rather let my poems do the talking. This first one's called 'Argile.'" He opens his notebook and clears his throat.

Pop, pop,
said Uncle Sam.
Pop, pop.
That's all you'll ever be.
A shadow of a legacy
stretching wide from sea
to sea.
Pop, pop.
Too clearly
I now can see.
My mind is free.
To be the me
I need
to be.
Pop, pop, Argile Pepinpopper.
Pop, pop.

The audience snaps it up, they really love this one, and Pete's most dedicated fans quietly squabble over who's heard him read it the most times. Pete waits for them to simmer down, then starts his next poem.

In the end, Pete reads for a full twenty-five minutes, far longer than any other reader, and his final poem is met not with snaps, but applause. When he's done, half the crowd surrounds him as he descends from the stage, congratulating him as they prepare to leave—after all, who else was anyone really here to see? But wait! The show's not over. Pete wants to see this next guy. A skinny overdressed Mexican man walks onstage despite the MC's warnings that he'll be crushed, that there's no way he can follow up Pete's electric performance! Seeing as Pete's sticking around, the audience half-heartedly gives José their divided attention.

"Hola," says José, grinning sheepishly.

The crowd yawns.

"I'm going to read some poems for you. They come from my heart." José begins with a subtle, tranquil poem about the sadness that weighed upon his heart when he saw how his cigarette habit hurt his mama. A hush falls over the crowd like midnight snow. A couple poems later they're hooked. José's words resonate with them on a deeper level than they've ever experienced. It's not about the spotlight, the fame, the immortal glory attainable only in coffeeshop open mics! No! This man has lived life and felt pain like no one else! Yet how is it possible that his poems are so universal? Almost everyone catches a glimpse of the overwhelming complexity of life and grasps the insignificance of their existence in the unfeeling universe while simultaneously gaining a deeper appreciation of the importance of their roles in the lives of their loved ones and even the lives of strangers.

Everyone, that is, except for Pete. The importance he has enjoyed for so long is light drowning beneath a rising horizon. To stop José would be akin to reversing the rotation of the Earth, but he has to try.

"Hey!" Pete shouts betwixt two phrases so pure, thine ears would seek deafness, for no sound uttered by man or woman, beast or nature could compare in beauty.

The crowd wavers between interest and anger.

Pete points a nicotine-stained finger at the stage. "I know that guy! Yeah, I knew José back in high school and, like, he totally failed poetry class!"

Gasps. The implications are clear. There's no way someone who failed high school poetry could write verse so divinely human. José must be a fraud! The crowd boos. Rotten vegetables machine gun across the stage and José dashes for the side door, narrowly avoiding the botanical onslaught. He sprints down the cool alley and out onto the moonlit street. He should be terrified of the crowd, their disapproval should have crushed him, but as he runs for his life, he feels a kind of freedom he hasn't felt since… who knows? He steps into the first bar he sees for a celebratory drink.

"One drink, please!"

The paunchy bartender grins. "One drink, comin' right up!"

José is starting to feel good about this city, smiles at the muchachos yammering away in Spanish a couple seats over. The bartender returns with José's celebratory drink. He takes a long gulp. Billiard balls clack in the artificial twilight. A poster for a brand of tequila hangs above the bar, its cheerful sombrero-clad cactus mismatching the atmosphere. There's something familiar about this place, but José can't quite put his finger on it. Then he turns to the bartender.

"Say, don't I know you?"

The bartender scratches his stubble and glances at the ceiling. Then he remembers and snaps his fingers.

"That's right! You helped fix my TV back at the old place!"

"I also shot three bandits," says José.

"Can't say I recall."

"Well it happened."

"Whatever you say." The bartender shakes his head and wipes down the bar and José catches on. Better to leave those bodies buried.

The exhausted MC droops into the room and orders the perfect drink to polish off a long, hard day.

"Looks like it's been a long day for both of us," he says to José.

"I suppose."

"You alright?"

José nods and takes a sip. "Wasn't so bad."

"What'd you do to piss off Pete?"

"He told me he was living in the shadow and light of that popcorn guy and I told him he wasn't."

The MC sighs. "That'll do it."

The bartender interjects. "You boys don't mean Pete the Poet, do ya?"

"Yep."

"Hate to tell you, pal, but your poetry career is over if you can't make things right with him."

José looks to the MC for answers.

"Afraid he's right. I don't think you understand the influence Pete has on the open mics around here. You're blacklisted."

"Dios mio." José drains his drink right as a fly buzzes in. With frog-like reflexes, José slams his glass down around the pest. For just a moment, the fly is trapped, its life surely finished. But the glass fissures and explodes and the fly escapes, deftly navigating the airborne shards like a space hero through an asteroid field.

"I'm so sorry—"

"Get out!" shouts the bartender.

"I'll clean—"

"Out!"

Tears in his eyes, José gets up and leaves. Outside, the street has lost its magic, and the wind blows dust behind his teeth.

The bar door swings open and the MC runs after him.

"José, wait up!"

José sucks it up and turns around. "What?"

The MC catches up and bends over panting, his hands on his knees. "Look, things might seem dire for your poetry career, but it doesn't have to be this way." He catches his breath and stands up straight. "Now Pete's ego might be easily bruised, but it's also easily mended. A simple apology in the form of a poetic elegy praising his valiant struggle against the legacy of Argile Peppinpopper has a very good chance of changing his mind."

José shakes his head. "I could never do that, because it wouldn't be true. Pete's a fool, and so long as he believes himself to be living in the shadow of the Popcorn Tycoon, there he shall remain."

"Don't you get it?" the MC asks, his voice cracking with desperation. "This isn't about the truth, damn it! It's about doing what it takes to be a poet! Sometimes you've gotta suck it up and say what you've gotta say or you'll never make it in this town!"

"I'm sorry, but I just can't."

The MC shakes his head. "You're making a big mistake." He takes out his notepad, scribbles something on it, and rips out the page. "Here's my number. Think about it."

José waves his hand to decline. "When I make a decision, I make it without hesitation. I am sure that this has hurt me many times, but to allow hesitation to creep back into my life would herald a return to pain far worse than anything I've experienced since I decided to stop hesitating."

The MC sighs. "Well, alright." He gives José a bold hug and bids him farewell.

On the walk back to his apartment José is assaulted from behind by a man in a basketball jersey. Though the city life has dulled his desert reflexes, José fights him off, then he fights off the next guy and does battle with dozens of other amateur ninjas, ordinary folks compelled by some unknown force to jump out of cars and alleyways, to run out of stores and leap from trees, kicking and laughing.

José climbs a fire escape and tries to pull the ladder up behind him, but his assailants are too fast and climb up after him. He scrambles higher and higher until he reaches the roof. Someone whistles and the mob coagulates into a liquid boot. The boot looms high above the rooftops and the moon shines through it. José strikes the toughest pose he knows, and in doing so feels a piece of paper stuck to the back of his shirt. The boot crashes down to smash him into blood, but stops midair when José removes the note. It reads "kick me," and below it is the MC's phone number. Prank over, the boot dissipates and its members stumble back to their lives, already forgetting their parts in something so great and terrible.

José wants to crumple the paper, but can't bring himself to do it. The MC truly wishes to help him, and in writing "kick me" above his number, he's shown José that if he doesn't take help when it's offered, this city will tear him apart. Paper in hand, José takes the long way home, leaping from roof to roof, jumping through his apartment window and landing next to his phone. He picks up the receiver and dials.

6

Michael's back in Leroy's office again, supposedly to talk business, but really he's just wasting time making pointless chit-chat. Leroy really ought to find a new vice president. Outside, dark clouds gather over the sea as Michael launches into some spiel about Piccadilly Willy, or maybe his son. Neither of them are sure, because neither of them know much about country music. Michael just thinks he's impressing Leroy.

"So like, I'm pretty sure without his influence, country-western never would have become what—"

"Where is this going Michael?"

Michael squeaks like a prom queen who's not on board with giving her crown to a hardworking disabled girl. "Jeez, Leroy, I'm just making conversation."

"Well how about you go make some money instead?"

Michael's shocked. Leroy never talks to him this way.

"Alright, I'm on it." Spirits low, Michael shuffles back to his desk. A subordinate comes over to him with a problem and Michael explodes, really lets him have it. Holding back tears, the subordinate scurries away crying. His coworkers ask what's wrong and he tells them and they feel for him and swap Michael stories and go out for drinks and start a band called The Winds of Justice. Soon they've got a hit single about their work troubles. While Michael or Saguaro Sombrero Solutions Unlimited aren't mentioned by name, anyone in the know can tell what it's about right away. The song becomes an underground sensation and soon it's playing during rush hour on 111.1, LA's Most Alternative Station. And thus it reaches the ears of a man named Arbuckle, the tech whiz in charge of Saguaro Sombrero Solutions Unlimited's computer systems. He can't believe what he's hearing, the song's describing all sorts of company drama to a tee. Back home at his personal computer, Arbuckle does some sleuthing and sure enough, the members of The Winds of Justice all work at Saguaro Sombrero Solutions Unlimited. Utilizing the company's state of the art electronic mail delivery system, Arbuckle spreads the word to all who might be sympathetic to The Winds of Justice's secret message. And so it begins.

Michael feels his authority slipping. Paralyzed like an overburdened dog walker, he watches the tide of anger wash over the office, growing louder and larger until it threatens to drown him. He makes a break for the men's restroom, grabs a mop, and locks himself in a stall just as the entire office floods in after him. Crouched low on the toilet seat, Michael beats back the clawing masses reaching under the door, silently thanking José for his insistence on strong locks and hinges on every stall due to some kind of traumatic experience to which he only alluded. Nevertheless, as strong as the lock is, it's starting to bend. Michael raises the mop handle like a dagger and stabs it through a pipe. He pulls it out and water gushes, breaking down the door from the inside and launching him high over the mob upon a triumphant wave. Door as his board, Michael surfs his way across half the office until the wave crashes. He kicks off the top, does a gnarly flip, and sticks the landing. The soaked drones stumble back to life and Michael sprints into Leroy's office and locks the door. When he realizes he's interrupting an Important Meeting with the Important Client, he wishes he'd let the mob take him.

"Can I help you, Michael?" Leroy asks, eyebrows raised.

The Important Client smirks and twists his moustache, relishing his position above the conflict.

Before Michael can answer, the office shakes like a ship in a tempest as the mob slams against the wall. Dust and plaster fall from the ceiling, furniture slides across the room, and the Important Client bursts into laughter.

"I warned you, McMenahan!"

"But I've been good to these people! I pay them well, I treat them right!"

Michael looks at his shoes, relieved the blame hasn't fallen on him, still nervous it might.

The Important Client strikes a match and lights a cigarillo. "After all my mentorship, you still blind yourself to the reality of the world. In our imperfect society, there are Creators, and there are parasites—"

"Am I a Creator?" asks Michael, glowing with hope.

"I don't know you," says the Important Client.

Michael collapses into a chair.

The Important Client rolls his eyes. "Who's responsible for this fiasco, whatever your name is?"

Michael's lips flap uselessly for a minute before he's able to speak. "Papapabapabapabapabapitts, it's, it's the whole, it's everyone, sir!"

Leroy throws his hat on the ground.

The Important Client chuckles. "Relax, McMenahan. I've been in this situation many times." The building shudders and the lights flicker. The shouts outside grow louder. "You say you paid these people well and treated them right. I have absolute confidence this is true."

"Then why is this happening?" asks Leroy.

"For the specific causes, we might ask this sad excuse of a man."

The Important Client's words hit Michael like a dump truck. He slips out of his chair and slumps face-down on the floor.

"There's no doubt in my mind that this fellow is to blame. Though he has admitted nothing, just look at how the weight of his actions crushes him."

Leroy has to admit, Michael isn't looking so hot right now. "Get up, Michael. Tell us what happened."

"I don't want to!"

Leroy lifts his boot, ready to stomp on him, but the Important Client shakes his head.

"Leave him be, McMenahan. I don't know what mistakes he's made, but I can guarantee they were not as critical as yours."

"And what might that be?" asks Leroy, his head spinning, shocked at what he almost did.

"You treated parasites as Creators. When underpaid workers strike, they strike for money. But what you have here is something different. These people are comfortable in their homes. They have no trouble feeding their families, sending their children to private schools, wasting company time on lavish vacations. You have given them happiness, but happiness is an illusion, and they are beginning to realize that the only thing worth having in this world is power. With one pursuit finished, another has begun."

The walls of the office bulge inward.

"Then what do I do?"

The Important Client blows two smoke rings and fires a smoke bullet through them. "Things may look dire now, but you're a Creator, just like me. Use this as an opportunity."

"For what?"

"I thought a fellow Creator would know an opportunity when he saw it. Michael, is it?"

Michael sits up, the color returning to his face. "Yes, sir."

"Who instigated this fiasco?"

"I don't know, sir, everyone just—"

"Everyone did not just spontaneously coagulate into a blob of rage. Think, Michael. Who might their leader be?"

Michael thinks about it. "If I could point to anyone, it would be Arbuckle."

"Arbuckle. A strong name. What does he do?"

"He's in charge of the computers. I heard there was some kind of electronic message he sent out that riled everyone up."

Leroy's heard of these computers, but he ain't exactly sure what they do. He reckons this Arbuckle fellow will be a tough sucker to tangle with.

"Well then, Michael," says the Important Client. "You must go out there and bring this Arbuckle in to speak with us."

Michael shakes his head so hard his hair almost falls out. "No way! They'll kill me!"

The Important Client chuckles. "No they won't. These are people accustomed to luxury, not killing. As a man accustomed to both, I can tell these things."

After some more convincing, Michael agrees to talk to the mob. He slips out and Leroy slams the door behind him. Gunshots. Screams. The Important Client realizes his folly and radios his personal helicopter. The walls look ready to snap in two.

"Let me in! Let me in!" Michael presses his face through the gap between the bending door and its frame, his shirt collar soaked in blood. Leroy grabs his arm. The helicopter arrives and the Important Client pries open a twisted window.

"Leave him, McMenahan!"

"Don't leave me!"

"I won't!" shouts Leroy, but he loses his grip and Michael's sucked back into the crowd. The lights cut out and chunks of ceiling fall from above. Leroy runs through the debris, scoops up his hat, leaps out the window and joins the Important Client on the rope ladder dangling down the side of the building. The chopper flies away and they hang tight, watching the smoke rise.

7

In the alley behind the coffeeshop, José crouches beneath the steel lid of a half-empty trash can. He wishes he'd emptied the trash into the dumpster before climbing in, but like the patient turtle, he cannot emerge from his shell until the danger has passed. The back door opens and out comes Pete and the MC. Pete pops a cigarette in his mouth and the MC lights it with both hands. José's throat itches and he swallows every drop of spit he can muster.

"I saw a girl eating popcorn," says Pete.

The MC turns pale. "No, I'm sure she was just—"

"Are you calling me a liar?"

The MC crushes some gravel under his shoe. "No, that's not what I meant."

"Then what did you mean?"

"I meant I'll go investigate."

"You won't just investigate, you'll deal with her. My nerves are fried enough as it is."

"Alright, Pete." The MC disappears back inside.

Pete takes a deep satisfied drag and cackles as he exhales. "It's good to be on top, baby. You're gonna kill it up there, Pete. And besides, Argile can't live forever." He grows quiet and thinks of all the things he'll say to the old man on the day their paths finally cross. But for each jagged stab of his wit, Argile has a kind and perfect response that deflects Pete's insults right back at him. In his heart, Pete knows Argile has no pride to defend, and that his anger is directed at a phantom. But this only makes him angrier, and he wishes there were a popcorn stand nearby so he could flip it over and stomp it all into smithereens.

48

He throws his cigarette on the ground just as the MC returns.

"The popcorn's gone."

"Good." Pete storms back inside.

When the door clicks shut, the MC gives José the signal. He climbs out and kicks the trash off his legs.

"Do you think anyone will notice the stains?"

The MC laughs. "Besides me, you're still the best-dressed hombre on the block."

José doesn't buy it, but knows his words are what will matter most.

"Here. Put these on." The MC hands him a classic nose-moustache-glasses disguise. José puts it on and it's perfect. There's no way anyone will recognize him before the critical moment. The MC opens the door.

"Wait!"

"What?"

"Does this place have an upright bass?"

The MC rolls his eyes. "José, it's a coffeeshop. Of course it does."

"Can you play it?"

"What does it matter?"

José grabs him by the shoulders. "This'll only work if you're on bass—and not only do I know you can play, I know you're good." He pulls out a record of some of his favorite poets reading their work, backed by The Friends of Poets Backing Band, a legendary group who, at the apex of their careers, disappeared without a trace—until now. For on the cover of the record, the MC himself is on bass, lost in a trance as Banks Nwokeji reads his famous poem, "Faxing Documents and Acquiring Credit Cards: The Modern Road to Success."

The MC shakes his head. "I haven't played in years, not since—"

"Not since Pete told you to stop?"

The MC stares at his shoes.

"Yeah, I asked around. I heard what happened." José shakes him. "Have some self respect, man! You're John fucking Smith! Pete got booed that night because his poems were bad, not because of you!"

The MC sniffs. "I know. But Pete'll never let me MC again if I play tonight!"

"Well I've got some good news for you, amigo. If we pull this off, you'll never have to take orders from Pete ever again."

The MC's terrified, but he can't hide from the truth—José's right. Someone has to stand up to Pete, and if it isn't them, then who? If not today, then when? Time slows to a crawl. A car whooshes down the empty street. The rattling air conditioner shifts into his awareness. The low hum of an airplane glues it all together and John Smith hears the music of the world once more.

"Alright. I'm in."

John and José take the stage and murmurs leap from the crowd like salmon as folks see through José's disguise and recognize him as the poet who crossed Pete. Everyone's shocked he has the guts to come back after the thrashing they gave him, but even more shocking is he got John fucking Smith to come out of musical retirement to back him up. Fortunately John put José's set in slot seventeen, the slot Pete always takes his bathroom break during, so no one feels pressured to start heckling. José steps up to the mic and John puts his fingers on the bass. The sound of a coin flipping echoes over the quiet crowd. It's a calming sound that represents odds better than José possesses. John plays an F sharp, one of the most interesting notes of all, followed by a G flat, a tasteful continuation. José begins an epic poem, written in the impressively difficult terza rima form, about the son of the man who invented lip balm. John fills in the spaces between words like the soft, expected bounce of a tennis ball upon the court after it's hit, and the audience soon realizes the poem is a metaphor for Massimiliano I's rise and fall from power as the only emperor of Mexico. The lighting guy dims the lights to match the mood and gives José a thumbs up, and as this final element of the ideal poetic atmosphere falls into place, it dawns on the audience that behind José's allusions to Massimiliano I lies a critique of another grand figure closer to home. The toilet flushes.

As he leaves the bathroom, Pete pretends to dry his hands off by wiping them on his pants. Stupid etiquette, if he didn't get any piss or shit on himself then what's the point of washing up? To provide cover for the slobs of the world? If so, the slobs have won, because he would die from embarrassment if anyone ever called him out on his hygiene.

But when no one even glances at his lavatorial emergence, Pete knows something's amiss, and when he sees José on stage wearing a stupid disguise, his blood boils all the bathroom germs right off. The crowd is hypnotized like moths to a flame, like deer in the headlights, like mosquitos to a mosquito lamp, like fish to an anglerfish—Pete's poetic mind races and stumbles and falls into clichés and isomorphic similes, clawing against the truth that the world that was beautiful and his has been fouled and desecrated beyond all hope of cleansing. Doesn't José realize he's destroying everything Pete's worked for, dethroning him, relegating him to the status of a mere participant? A firmament opens and Pete sees himself cast into the dustbins of poetic history, a footnote in the monumental life of José Jones. Pete stumbles and clutches a wooden column, hugging it with both arms and sliding to a crouch. Such beauty! Such truth! He has to leave. Were he to stay, he could do nothing but debase himself, admit he was wrong, that José is the better poet, the better man. A shadow falls over him and he looks up past the well-shined shoes of the tall old man looming overhead, silhouetted in the dim light.

"You'll never live up to my legacy, Pete. You never even got halfway. You're done, boy. Finished!" says Argile.

"No!" Pete shouts. "I'm not done yet! The world hasn't seen the last of Pete the Poet!" The people nearby shush him and he stands up on wobbly knees and bolts for the door. He hears Argile laugh and stretch taller behind him, smells the popcorn on his breath, jostles through the bobo dolls and out of the coffeeshop and runs down the dark street, menaced by a presence far more terrifying than a vegetable-toting mob.

8

Back at his compound, the Important Client calls his good friend, the Chief of Police, and half the cops in town surround the office of Saguaro Sombrero Solutions Unlimited. The workers have taken up strategic posts throughout the smoking wreckage, and the police are concerned that any attempt to breach the premises might result in the building's total collapse. So they wait outside, prepared to starve them out. At dusk the Chief gets a call from a scrambled voice identifying itself as "The Prince of Danger." The Prince declares that the workers have claimed the company for themselves, and asks law enforcement to respect the due process of laissez-faire capitalism and let the executives of Saguaro Sombrero Solutions Unlimited take it back if they are worthy. The Chief chews his donut thoughtfully, decides he'd better call his boss.

"They're workers, and they're using big words, but they're the same big words you're usually using. You know, talking about lacy fairs and such. They're talking about the company like, well, they're telling you to come and take it. And that reminds me of that famous flag, the one that says COME AND TAKE IT on it. It's an American flag, and that gets my blood pumping. But they're also breaking the law, so I just don't know what to do here, sir." Exasperated, the Chief of Police rewards himself with a donut-sized bite of another donut.

The Important Client takes a long drag of his cigarillo, then bursts into laughter. "Don't those fools understand?

We're thick as thieves, you and I. The police force isn't some unbiased executor of blind justice! No offense."

"None taken."

"They may have confused you by adopting the nomenclature of us Creators, but pay no mind to their cheap ruse—this is no different from any other parasitic uprising."

"What do you want us to do, though? There's no way we're getting in there without a fight—a big one. We're gonna lose people, sir."

The Important Client covers his mic. "What do you think, Leroy?"

Leroy looks up from his sudoku. "They've stationed their cannon, and I reckon I'll take it."

"You're a damn fool, Leroy. But a brave one. It's what us Creators have got to be to Create in this world of parasites."

Tired of all this talk of Creators and parasites, Leroy says nothing.

The Important Client uncovers his mic. "We're going in, I'm sending Leroy over."

"Who?"

"Leroy McMenahan, CEO of Saguaro Sombrero Solutions Unlimited, that's who! Await his instructions." The Important Client hangs up and stubs his cigarillo in the soil of a potted fern. "Don't be too hard on yourself, McMenahan. I myself made a critical blunder in managing our partnership. Shall I tell you?"

"Reckon I already know."

The Important Client smirks. "Is that so? Go on."

"You blew smoke on my friend's bonsai tree."

This isn't what the Important Client had in mind, but it's the correct answer. Leroy leaves before the bewildered tycoon can dredge up the forgotten incident.

Leroy pulls into the cordoned parking lot and is stopped by some cops at the perimeter. He rolls his window down.

"I'm Leroy. The Chief's expecting me."

The cops are suspicious, but one of them radios the Chief and sure enough, Leroy gets the green light. He drives through the rows of parked cruisers until the Chief waves him down. He parks and steps out.

"What's the situation?"

"Bad." The Chief points to the building with a sandwich wrapped in wax paper. "They've got the whole place covered. There's no way in without a fight."

"Is that so? What about—"

"Let me walk you through it." The Chief points out every spot the workers have covered, illustrates every angle of approach and why it won't work, pre-empting all of Leroy's questions.

Leroy whistles. "Well I'll be. This is a doozy, alright."

"That's for sure. Seems like the only thing to do is starve 'em out," says the Chief, taking a bite of his pastrami melt.

Leroy's thinking gears start turning.

"What are you thinking about?"

"I reckon there's something y'all ain't thought of."

It's not easy, but after a long and complicated plan involving distractions, the sewer system, and a whole lot of luck, Leroy pops out of an air duct into the abandoned food court. The Burrito Bell is cracked, the Micky Ronaldinio's M is an epsilon, and the Carlos Jr. has lost its innocence. The building shakes and dust falls from the ceiling. Leroy walks across the tiles, his footsteps echoing. When he notices a blinking security camera, loudspeakers crackle to life.

"Welcome back to Saguaro Sombrero Solutions Unlimited, Leroy!"

"Arbuckle!" he shouts.

"Well, well, well, you know who I am. But come on, Leroy, I'm the one calling the shots here. You should call me Mr. Arbuckle!"

"And you should call me Mr. McMenahan!"

"I don't think so. See you at the top—if you're still alive!" Arbuckle cackles and signs off.

It'll be a long, hard climb, so Leroy reckons he ought to partake in some sustenance before he makes the trek. He weighs his options before stepping behind the counter of Carlos Jr. He washes his hands and eats a cold cheeseburger sitting on the counter. It's a big burger, and he might have bitten off more than he can chew. He spots a conspicuous pile of trays in the corner of the kitchen right as it explodes and charges at him. Like an air dancer at a used car dealership, Leroy dodges his assailant and grabs him by the wrist.

"Not today!"

The pudgy boy starts blubbering and crying. "I'm sorry! Please don't take me to the Prince of Danger!"

Realizing he's dealing with a scared kid, Leroy lets him go.

"Don't worry, I ain't one of them."

"Oh, thank God." The boy leans against the counter and catches his breath.

"Carlos, sir." The boy points up at the sign. "No relation."

"Leroy," says Leroy, extending his hand. "Pleasure to meet you."

They shake hands, then Carlos' eyes go wide. "Wait a second. You don't mean—you're Leroy McMenahan?"

"That's me."

"You're a living legend!"

Leroy smirks. "And what did I do to deserve that insult?"

"You're in, like, half the examples of good business practices in my textbook!" Carlos pulls the book out and points to a black and white photo of Leroy cutting the grand opening ribbon at the first Saguaro Sombrero Solutions Unlimited factory. A tanned hand reaches into the photo and holds the ribbon taught. "Everything I ever learned about business, I learned from you. I'm planning on opening my own burger joint one day! I hope you'll pay me a visit."

"You can count on it Carlos," says Leroy, flipping through the book. "But your book sure has a lot of misconceptions about my company."

Carlos looks worried, like a child realizing he's about to be told Santa isn't real. "Like what?"

"Well for one, there isn't anything about José in here."

"Who's José?"

"Who's José!" Leroy throws his hat on the ground. "Without José Jones, this company wouldn't exist!" The building rumbles.

"No offense, Mr. McMenahan, but does your company still exist?"

"Exactly. Things ain't been right ever since José left." He puts his hat back on. "But as long as this building's still standing, I can't give up. I can't let some computer nerd and his goons get the best of me."

"Then let me help you. I know a thing or two about computers and I'm a green belt in karate! Hi-ya!" Carlos shows off some moves.

"Kid, don't put yourself in danger just 'cause someone wrote some nice things about me in a book."

Carlos laughs. "Please, those jerks upstairs treat me like crap every day and now they're gonna wreck this place and I'm gonna lose my job. So if you don't think I've got a dog in this fight, think again. Hoowagh!" Carlos thrusts into the Tranquil Lotus fighting stance, but Leroy's already started towards the stairs.

After only a few floors, Carlos is too winded to continue. He stops to rest.

Leroy looks back and sighs. "I ain't gonna wait up for you, Carlos!"

"Sorry, Mr. McMenahan. I'll catch up later."

Leroy shakes his head. He didn't sign up to be a babysitter. He keeps climbing until he's blocked by a pile of rubble.

"Damn it!" Leroy looks down the stairwell shaft, down through squares and squares converging to infinity. "Carlos! How far are you?" He hears his voice ping pong like a coin bouncing down a deep well.

Carlos' voice echoes back up, but the reverberation obscures the words.

"What was that?"

Carlos answers again, but Leroy still can't understand him. He leaves his bandana behind as a marker, then opens the door and enters the nineteenth floor.

A deserted office. Some fallen chairs and scattered papers, but otherwise as it would be after-hours. The bulletin board displays the usual announcements regarding company potlucks and sales quotas, but also flyers calling for shorter hours, an end to bullying, and for Leroy to say goodnight. He's not sure what to make of this last flyer until he hears wind and ducks just in time to dodge a baseball bat. He kicks out behind him and lodges his spur in the assailant's knee. The goon shouts and breaks away from Leroy, swinging again and hitting him in the ribs.

Leroy crashes to the carpet and rolls under a desk like a golf ball into a cup and the bat comes down again, splitting the desk in two, landing in Leroy's hands. He struggles to keep the bat up until the thug changes his strategy and yanks it away. Leroy gets up and faces his enemy.

"Remember me, Leroy?" The man's wearing a dark pinstriped suit with a rose pinned to the chest. His eyes are hidden behind impenetrable sunglasses and his black hair is slicked back.

"I recognize your face. But I reckon I won't after this."

Bat over his shoulder, the man smirks. "I was in charge of the ad campaign for that tequila deal. And these," he arcs his bat around the room. "Are my associates." Salarymen emerge from behind desks and potted plants, a few even jump down from ceiling panels. "Why don't you quit while you can?"

"You think this is enough to make me quit?"

The ad man laughs. "Oh you aren't quitting, Leroy. You're fired! We made this company, we made you. Without us, no one would know your name. And now it's our time to—"

Suddenly half the salarymen fall, blood spurting from gashes in their arms, chests, and necks. A soggy red paper airplane circles the room and lands gently in Carlos' hand.

"I forgot to mention that my dojo specializes in white collar combat."

"Carlos!"

The ad man grits his teeth. "Get him!"

Leroy and Carlos stand back to back and fend off the first few attackers. Carlos grabs a floor lamp and takes on five goons at once. Leroy fights mano a mano with the ad man. They block and dodge each other's blows, each thinking ten moves ahead. After two incredible flying kicks collide midair, they backflip away from each other and land on their feet.

"Not bad for a cowboy," says the ad man.

"I ain't had a fight this good in a long—" Leroy is interrupted by the crack of Carlos' lamp on the back of the ad man's skull. His eyes roll back into his head and he drops to the floor. Leroy turns around and gazes at the pile of bodies. "You did good, Carlos."

"Thanks, boss. I guess all that training came in handy." Carlos blushes and scratches the back of his head.

That was more than just training.

"Let's keep moving," says Leroy. The duo forge through the office and wheeze up ten more flights of stairs.

"This seems too easy," says Carlos. "Besides these stairs, of course."

A loudspeaker crackles.

"Don't you worry," says Arbuckle. "It's about to get a whole lot harder. Why don't you pay me a visit on the next floor?" He cackles and disconnects.

"I've got a bad feeling about this," says Carlos.

"Don't worry. Arbuckle may be a whiz at those computers, but he won't stand a chance against the old one-two!" Leroy punches the air. "Let's go!"

They enter the next room. It's empty, white, and large as a gymnasium. The door locks behind them, the lights cut out, and a green neon grid spreads out across the floor, walls, and ceiling. A purple cube appears by the exit, then expands into four cubes, then sixteen, until Leroy and Carlos find themselves confronted by a jagged, geometric bull. Twenty feet tall, it snorts data and scrapes its virtual foot on the ground. Leroy snaps into a powerful fighting stance. A translucent, holographic Arbuckle appears midair.

"Welcome to cyberspace!" he says.

60

"Cyberspace? What's going on here, Arbuckle?" shouts Leroy.

"While you fools were busy with the advertising department, I was programming your downfall. T.A.U.R.O.S! Destroy them!" The bull roars and charges. Leroy and Carlos jump away and the bull runs between them into the wall. It turns around and scrapes its hoof on the ground, preparing to charge again.

Arbuckle cackles. "T.A.U.R.O.S. is far too mighty even for you, Leroy! Run all you want, it won't do you any good!"

The bull charges again. Leroy jumps up and lands on its nose, but it shakes him off and he smacks into a wall. He slides down to the floor and the bull charges at Carlos. Looking for a place to run, Carlos spots an old terminal by the exit.

"Leroy!" he shouts. "If you distract T.A.U.R.O.S. I think I can use that terminal to stop him!"

Leroy stands up and dusts himself off. "What do you mean?"

"I've taken a couple computing classes at community college. I'm not the best programmer, but if I can hack into Arbuckle's system and override the database mainframe, I just might be able to shut this program down and get us out of here!"

"I didn't understand a word you just said, Carlos, but I trust you. Let's get a move on!"

Right as the bull's about to trample Carlos, he cartwheels off to the side and over to the terminal.

"Hey, over here!" shouts Leroy, waving his hat. The bull turns and charges at him. Leroy kicks off the wall and jumps across the room. Carlos starts hacking.

"I'm the greatest programmer I've ever met," says Arbuckle. "There's no way you can hack into my system!"

"We'll see about that, Arbuckle," says Carlos, typing up a storm. "There, I've logged in."

Arbuckle folds his arms and floats closer to Carlos. "Impressive. But you'll never crack my encryption wall!"

Carlos' fingers are a blur, the keyboard clatters like plastic rain. He hits enter and torrents of green text pour down the screen. "Looks like I just did."

Arbuckle breaks a sweat. "Impossible!"

The bull charges and Leroy kicks it in the side of the face. It swerves and shakes itself off.

"Yeehaw!"

"Uh-oh," says Carlos. "I've never seen this kind of data before!"

Arbuckle breathes a sigh of relief. "That's because you're just a stupid kid in way over your head. Looks like you're not ready to play ball with the big boys."

"Don't be so sure about that, Arbuckle!" shouts Leroy, knocking the bull up into the air with a swift uppercut. "That kid's got more spirit in his pinky than you've got in your whole soul!"

"Spirit doesn't mean a thing in cyberspace!" says Arbuckle. The bull gets up with great effort. "It seems T.A.U.R.O.S. could use a little help. Computer! Rejuvenate life points! Increase strength values! Maximize speed!" The bull glows and grows even larger. Its shadow stretches across the grid and covers Leroy.

"Come on, Carlos, hurry it up now," says Leroy, backing away. The bull teleports across the room and knocks Leroy into the air.

Carlos types faster. "I'm almost there. I just have three more firewalls to break through."

"Each one harder than the last," says Arbuckle, stroking his hairy chin. "By the time you even crack the first, both of you will be hanging from T.A.U.R.O.S.' horns!"

The bull raises a hoof and swats Leroy into the wall. Leroy slides down like egg on a windshield.

"You're right," says Carlos. "As things stand, hacking these firewalls will take too long. Unless I give Leroy a boost!"

A suit of robotic armor materializes around Leroy, his right arm morphing into a blaster.

"Now go get him, Leroy!"

Leroy stands up on shaky legs, charges his blaster, and shouts with all his might as he shoots out a massive energy beam, pinning the bull to the wall and rippling the grid.

"No!" shouts Arbuckle. "That's not allowed! Computer! Generate three more T.A.U.R.O.S." Three cubes materialize and unfold into identical bulls. They each charge at Leroy, but he blasts them all away with ease.

"I've broken through the first firewall!" says Carlos.

"Not bad," says Arbuckle. "But the next two are impossible to crack."

Carlos types for a second. "He's right, Leroy. This next one alone is far beyond my capabilities."

Leroy fires a shot at Arbuckle, but it passes straight through him.

"Tsk, tsk, Leroy. That's no way to treat your host. Now, time to end this. Computer! Generate ninety-nine cyberdactyls!"

A flock of triangles expand and unfold into a seething mass. The cyberdactyls swoop and screech with all the speed and terror of their prehistoric counterparts. Then they start skipping frames and lagging. The grid blinks on and off.

"No!" cries Arbuckle. "Undo! Undo! Undo! Cancel! Reset!" The grid blinks off. Arbuckle and the cyberdactyls and Leroy's power suit vanish. The exit unlocks.

"Let's go!" shouts Carlos, jumping up with his fist raised. He runs through the door with his arms stretched behind and Leroy saunters after him, in awe of the beauty and power and savage indifference of technology.

9

Leroy and Carlos enter the control room, a dark space filled with flashing lights and beeping sounds, the walls lined with tall servers, the floor a labyrinth of desks and swivel chairs, snaking cables and computing equipment.

"Come on out, Arbuckle!" shouts Leroy. "We know you're in here."

There's no response. Carlos gives Leroy a silent gesture and they split up and patrol the room. Leroy checks under desks, untangles nests of wire, and sticks his head in the spaces between servers, but there's no sign of him.

"Leroy, I found something!"

Leroy runs over, tripping over cables and banging his knees a couple times along the way.

"Check this out." Carlos points at a terminal lit up with green text. It's a message from Arbuckle.

"Fools! You may have defeated T.A.U.R.O.S. and bypassed my firewalls, but you won't get your hands on me! I have successfully uploaded myself into cyberspace and by now I'm long gone. I could be on any computer in the world! Sayonara, suckers! P.S. Good luck getting through the control room's biometrically encrypted security system without my help!"

"Damn it!" shouts Leroy, crushing his hat in his fist. "What the hell are we supposed to do now?"

"I don't know," says Carlos. "They didn't teach us anything about this stuff in computer class."

Under the desk, someone sneezes.

"What was that?" asks Leroy.

Carlos bends down and pulls Arbuckle out kicking and screaming.

"Arbuckle!"

"Don't hurt me! I was just following orders, I swear!"

"Whose orders?" asks Leroy, holding him up by his shirt.

"The Prince of Danger!"

"The Prince of Danger?" asks Carlos.

"I heard about this guy," says Leroy. "Who the hell is he?"

Arbuckle grins. "You don't know?"

"Should I?"

"He's only your closest friend."

The idea of José being behind all this flashes through Leroy's mind, but he knows better. "Well in that case I reckon he won't object to us paying him a visit." He lets go and Arbuckle lands on his hands and knees, panting. Carlos kicks his ass.

"Get walking."

Arbuckle stumbles forward and leads them to the biometrically secured exit. "The Prince of Danger has grown quite powerful since you last saw him."

"Just open the door," says Leroy.

Arbuckle snorts. "Don't say I didn't warn you." He puts his eyeball to the scanner and a green light sweeps his retina. The doors hiss open and he scurries away.

Leroy looks Carlos in the eye. "You ready?"

"I was born ready."

They do a complicated improvised handshake that ends in a half-hug, then march down the long dark hallway.

Back at his compound, the Important Client has been watching everything in his surveillance room. He strokes his mustache and nods thoughtfully.

"Leroy's even more impressive than I thought. And that boy Carlos was a lucky discovery. Once again, I've invested quite well. But this Prince of Danger fellow—I'm intrigued. One never knows when one might need... let's say... no, let's not say. Let's see."

Leroy and Carlos reach the stairs leading up to the top floor.

"Welcome," says a voice. "So glad you've made it."

Leroy can't believe it. "That's not—it can't be—is that you, Michael?"

They summit the stairs and sure enough, it really is Michael dressed in all black with a cape and a pointy collar and triangular sunglasses, surrounded by a legion of Saguaro Sombrero Solutions Unlimited employees.

"Ah Leroy, still clinging to the past. They call me The Prince of Danger now, but you can call me CEO."

A dark wind rattles the windows.

"CEO? I'm the only CEO around here!"

Michael laughs and the legion laughs with him. "Not anymore, Leroy! This is my company now!"

"I don't get it. Were you unhappy as Vice President?"

"Unhappy? The best day of my life was the day you promoted me! It was only later when I learned of your abusive ways, always passing the buck to me when things went wrong, that I realized my duty to liberate this company."

"Abuse? Liberate? Why I've never passed the buck for anything in my entire life, period!"

The legion boos.

"My legion disagrees!"

"Michael, I treated you with nothing but respect! Even when you'd come into my office and bore the crap out of me with all your trivia about the Wild West and country music! I'm from out there, I'm sick of that stuff! Half of what you said was wrong anyways!"

Something's not adding up for the legion. These revelations about Michael's boring conversations are too specific to be lies.

"See?" says Michael. "We've hardly spoken two words and already you can't help but rehash your old petty grievances."

"You started it!"

"Hey Prince of Danger, you haven't been, uh, exaggerating about all that stuff Leroy did, have you?" asks one worker, a tall, upright man named Bartusz, polite but loyal only to the truth.

"How dare you suggest such a thing after all I've led you through, after all we've accomplished! We are inches away from defeating Leroy once and for all! Now is not the time for doubt!"

"Jeez, I was just asking. I don't appreciate getting yelled at like that."

"Yeah, that was out of line, Prince of Danger."

"What's your deal?"

The legion grows restless. Though some remain loyal to the Prince, they are increasingly overshadowed by those beginning to see him as another tyrant in the making, remembering that even though Leroy was in charge, he was never the one heaping abuse on them. It was always Michael. How could they ever have let him pass the buck for the way he treated them?

"The Prince of Danger's a fraud!"

"Get him!"

And just like that, the tide has turned. The crowd tries to grab Michael but he evades their clutches and runs out the door. They chase after him and end up on the roof just in time to watch him board a chopper. It takes off. Leroy pulls out a lasso and tosses it. It snags on one of the chopper's landing skids and he's yanked into the air.

"No, Leroy, let it go!" shouts Carlos, but it's too late, he's already over the edge.

"Come on everyone, if we band together we can save him!" shouts Bartusz. The crowd roars and everyone joins together into a hundred foot tall Mega Worker. The Mega Worker reaches its hand out and grabs Leroy and the rope. The chopper creaks as it threatens to capsize, but the rope snaps and Michael escapes into the storm. Safe on the roof, Leroy dusts himself off as the Mega Worker disbands.

"Whew," he says. "That was a doozy."

"We almost had him!" says Carlos.

"And we'll get him, alright. Don't you worry." Leroy slaps Carlos on the back.

"Hey, uh, Leroy?" asks Bartusz, scratching the back of his head. "We're sorry about all this. For real."

Leroy scans the crowd. Everyone's nodding with sincere regret. "Alright, I appreciate it," he says. "But y'all are liable for the damages."

"But Leroy, there's no way we can afford that!"

He thinks it over. "You know what, that wasn't fair of me. I never knew how bad things were for y'all, and I kept a diabolical number two around who grossly mistreated you and tried to stab me in the back. I'll pay for half."

Bartusz thinks about it. "It's a deal."

The workers cheer and Carlos whips up a contract on the fly. Everyone lines up to sign it with smiles on their faces, not realizing that once they take the time to do the math, they're all still gonna go bankrupt.

Michael gazes back at the smoldering office building, at the legion he just lost. He sheds a tear, then turns to the pilot.

"Who are you? Where are we going?"

"Relax, kid. You've made yourself a powerful friend."

"I have? Who?"

The pilot smirks. "You'll see."

10

And just like that, José is launched into stardom. Word of Pete's defeat spreads like a disease, killing off all reverence for the popcorn poet and replacing it with fanatic adulation of the sublime verse of the recently unknown man of the desert, his bourgeois past as co-CEO of Saguaro Sombrero Solutions Unlimited carefully concealed by his publishing house. Within no time, José's first collection tops the bestseller list, and his life whips into a whirlwind of poetry readings, high profile interviews, and exclusive workshops.

This evening finds him at the annual Los Angeles Poetry Guild Banquet, the most prestigious poetic gala in the whole city, if not the country, if not the world. This year's Poet of the Year is, of course, José Jones. He's not shocked, yet he's still overcome with emotion. He gets up from his table and walks over to the stage on shaky legs. Everyone stands up, applauding as he accepts his trophy, shakes the host's hand, and steps up to the mic.

"Wow. Just—wow. I don't know what to say. I'm lost for words, lost from pain and loneliness and silent suffering. I know we haven't all met, but I feel surrounded by family. You have no idea how much that means to me." He can't hold the tears back anymore and the applause grows louder, all the critics and poets and patrons of the arts brimming with admiration and gratitude for all José has done for the world.

An hour later, José's the life of the after party. Everyone wants a piece of him, they just can't help themselves. He's flattered but overwhelmed by all the adoring words, smiling faces, and grasping hands. Finally enough's enough. He excuses himself to the lavatory, pushes his way to the front of the line, and locks the door behind him. Free at last.

"Whoops."

José turns. A beautiful woman with an afro wearing a green canvas jacket is seated on the toilet with her cargo pants down. He covers his eyes and turns away.

"Lo siento! I didn't know you were in here!"

The woman smiles and wipes. "It's my bad. I forgot to lock the door." She stands up, puts her pants back on, and flushes the toilet. "You can look now."

José turns around, blushing. "I'm so sorry—"

"Hey, I said it was my bad. Besides, how else would I get a private meeting with José Jones?" She extends her hand. "Renée."

José almost shakes it, but hesitates. "Um—"

Renée's almost offended. "What?"

"Your—the sink?"

She laughs. "Of course." She washes her hands with soap, dries them off on a disgusting monogrammed hand towel, and finally they shake hands.

"Nice to meet you," says José.

"The pleasure's all mine."

José shakes his head. "Alone with a beautiful woman—I must disagree."

Renée rolls her eyes. "Do you flirt like this with all your lady fans?"

"No."

"Liar." She pushes him up against the door and sticks her tongue down his throat.

Sitting on the edge of the bed, wiping his dick off with tissues after three hours of passionate lovemaking, José can't help but wonder if this is going to go somewhere this

72

time, if he's growing too used to transient relationships, to melting the wings of angels flying too close to his poetic brilliance.

Renée lights a cigarette. "You want one?"

"Sure." He reaches over and takes one, ignoring his mama's pleas.

"Come lie back down."

José shakes his head. "I don't like getting ash on my chest." He lights it, then stands up, parts the curtains, and gazes out at the city.

"You really are a deep guy, aren't you?"

"No deeper than anyone else." He exhales smoke.

Renée sneaks up from behind and wraps her arms around him, her breasts pressed against his back, her delicate hands on his flat stomach.

"What's bothering you?"

"I... I don't know."

"Bullshit, you're a fucking poet! Of course you know!"

Cigarette in his mouth, José says nothing.

She slides her right hand down and grabs his balls. "Don't you trust me?"

"Yes," he says, wincing.

"Say si Mami."

"Si Mami."

She laughs and lets go, then walks back to the nightstand and resumes her cigarette.

Six months fly by and they're still at it. José calls her his muse and Renée calls him her dude. All the poems in his latest collection are about her, sometimes literally, sometimes metaphorically, always written with intensity and tenderness. Early reviews are already hailing *Poems About You, My Love* as an artistic breakthrough, a bold risk that has not only paid off, but solidified José as a chameleon comfortable writing in any style, a true visionary with an unmistakable voice, an honors roll student of the heart—in short, one of the Greats.

When José arrives at the Fighting Mambos Precinct #5 after a long day writing in his study, Renée greets him with a passionate kiss and a stack of reviews.

"Oh José, baby, they love it—I love it! Why didn't you tell me you were writing about me?"

José grins. "If I'd told you, you would have wanted to see them before they were finished, and I wouldn't have been able to resist."

"You know me too well." She squeezes him tight and he hugs her back, careful of the assault rifle slung across her shoulders. "Thank you."

"There's no need to thank me. The words flowed from my heart as naturally as breath from my lungs. Those poems are just an inevitable byproduct of our love."

She rolls her eyes. "So modest."

They head inside. The compound's bustling with activity. Committed freedom fighters stroll the halls, hold meetings in windowless rooms, shoot paper cops in the indoor firing range, study revolutionary theory and guerilla tactics in the people's library, and smoke weed and play ping pong and videogames in the lounge.

"Yo, what's good, José?" says Chairman Clyde, a brawny guy in cargo pants and a tank top sporting the Fighting Mambos logo, a fist with a mambo snake entwined around it, representing revolution and healing. Next to him, Anita, a shredded woman wearing the same outfit, is playing *Jumping Plumber* on the TV.

"Yo, what's up Clyde?" José and Clyde do their personal secret handshake and all the other fighters in the room acknowledge him with cool nods. José sits down in a comfy armchair and Renée drapes herself across his lap.

"What's the plan today?" she asks.

"Some comrades are trying to take over this factory just outside of town. That's cool, right?" he asks, turning to José.

"Yeah, of course," says José, not sure why Clyde's asking him.

Clyde looks into his eyes, searching for some kind of hidden reaction. "Yeah. Only problem is, the fat cat's in tight with the pigs. Already crushed an uprising at the white collar level and made those suckers pay big time. Word gets out that our comrades are making moves to get what they deserve, well, let's just say he ain't gonna be too happy about that."

"So that's where we come in," says Renée, cocking her rifle.

"We're gonna bring the revolution to these motherfuckers one factory at a time!" says Anita as she stomps on a lizard and raises the plumber's flag high above the castle.

"Most definitely. So you in or what?" Clyde asks.

"Of course! Sounds like fun," says José.

"Right on, brother." Clyde brings it on in for another secret handshake, and for the first time since he and Renée started dating, José feels like part of the gang.

The factory's all the way out in the desert just past the airplane graveyard. The Fighting Mambos roll up in black jeeps. A worker comrade opens the gate. A lot of other comrades are already outside holding signs, but it's pretty hot so they're all crowded together in the building's shadow. Cheers erupt when the Fighting Mambos arrive. Clyde gets out and raises his fist.

"Comrades! Let's win this fight!"

The workers raise their fists and burst into revolutionary song. The other Fighting Mambos get out and assume tactical positions around the premises. Randall, the leader of the workers, walks up to Clyde and gives him a soldier's hug.

"Clyde, my brother, you really came through."

"I wouldn't miss it. This is one righteous fucking cause y'all got going." He waves José and Renée over. "Randall, this is Renée and her boyfriend José."

Randall shakes both their hands. "Thanks for joining the cause."

"No need for thanks, brother," says Renée. "Clyde's been telling us all afternoon how underpaid and mistreated y'all are."

"Yeah and there's no AC in there! Honestly, if that's the only demand they meet, I'll be chilling. Literally!" He laughs.

Clyde puts his hand on Randall's shoulder. "Don't sell yourself short, brother. We'll get y'all everything y'all deserve!"

"Goddamnit, Clyde, this is why you're the man!"

In the midst of the comradery, José notices something that makes his stomach sink. Written in huge letters at the top of the factory is a familiar name: Saguaro Sombrero Solutions Unlimited. He's not sure what to do. He loves Renée, but without Leroy he never would have made it big in business and poetry, and they would never have met. Before he can make up his mind, cop cars roar through the desert and surround the workers, choppers swarming overhead.

"Get back to work!" commands a voice from on high. "Any further disobedience will be prosecuted to the fullest extent as trespassing and vandalism!"

The crowd boos.

"Pigs!" shouts Renée, aiming her rifle at the sky.

76

"No!" shouts José, but Renée opens fire and rips a chopper to shreds. It spirals to the Earth and explodes in a fiery plume.

"What are you doing?!" screams José.

"Protecting the workers! Don't be a pussy!" She laughs and unloads another stream of lead into the blue.

José pukes.

The cops pull barricades out of a big truck and fortify the perimeter.

The workers and Fighting Mambos close ranks.

"We need some motherfuckers on the roof!" shouts Clyde, giving the signal to Squadron Gamma.

The cops fire tear gas over the barricades and it's instant chaos. Everyone's coughing and crying, eyes stinging, colliding with each other in the crush through the factory doors.

"Seal it up!" Clyde shouts. In seconds every entrance is blocked off. Those not gassed as badly help the wounded recover, fetching rags and pouring water in their eyes.

Outside, the Chief of Police gets on the loudspeaker. "You have thirty minutes to come out with your hands up! We were willing to negotiate, but now that you've opened fire, we have no choice but to bring you in!"

"Pigs!" screams Renée, and the whole crowd jeers with her.

José knows what he needs to do. He climbs the stairs to the foreman's office and hunts around for the intercom. He thinks it's a big red button, but that just sets off an ear splitting alarm. He quickly turns it off and finds the right switch.

"Sorry about that," he says. "Wrong button."

Now he's got everyone's attention.

"José?" shouts Clyde.

"Please, everybody, please listen. Most of you may know me for my poetry, but what you don't know is that I was one of the two founders of this company. In fact, less than a year ago, I was still one of its joint CEOs."

The crowd boos.

"I understand how you feel, but please, hear me out!"

The disgruntled crowd reluctantly simmers down.

"Now I didn't leave this company to be a poet. Poetry's always been in my heart, and that'll never change. No, I left because I felt something was deeply wrong, that somewhere along the way, we'd lost our way. I was too high up to see any of your problems, but now I understand that I could feel them rippling up through the ranks, chilling my bones, unsettling my soul. Not to mention the damage inflicted upon my honor, my integrity, my self-esteem in my dealings with hollow people up at the top, monsters who care only for money, for luxury, for power, heartless fiends who have no appreciation for the simple things in life, an absolute necessity that no one can truly live without, for in its absence each rung climbed on the ladder of wealth and power causes the others to disintegrate beneath you, and you find yourself not on a ladder at all but a treadmill from which you cannot escape, cannot understand the meaning of, cannot feel the—" José stops and clears his throat, realizing he's losing them. "Those cops outside aren't here to protect you or hear your concerns. They're here for one thing—to protect the wealth of their corporate benefactors." The crowd roars in agreement. "And so I find myself in a unique position. I have all the connections of a business tycoon, and yet I've chosen to become a poet of the people. Let me fight for you! Give me a list of your demands and I'll go out there and make it happen!"

Some people are enthralled by José's rallying cry, but others are suspicious.

"How do we know we can trust you?"

"Yeah, what if he's a spy?"

Now half the crowd's jeering at him. José's not sure what to do. He puts his hand over his heart, about to say something about how they know his heart through his poetry, when Renée fires a few rounds into the ceiling.

"He's my boyfriend! You think I'd be dating him if he wasn't one hundred percent with the cause?"

No one can argue with that.

"Go on, José," says Clyde. "Show us what you got."

A list of demands in his pocket, a megaphone in his hand, José climbs out onto the roof. He walks out to the edge and stands in silhouette against the sky, one man against an army of cops, hair blowing in the wind like a messiah. He lifts the megaphone to his lips and holds down the button.

"Friends! Hear my words!"

"Who the hell is that?" asks a cop.

"I don't know, but we don't negotiate with terrorists," says another.

"My name is José Jones. I was once co-CEO—" A shot rings out and he falls back.

"Did he just say he was José Jones?"

"There's no way—"

"Well you better go check, cause if he is, and we just killed him—"

The cops get on the radio and have a chopper fly over the roof. Two commandos rappel down and inspect the body. It really is him. They radio the Chief who just about loses his lunch when he hears what happened. Hands shaking, he calls his boss.

"Mr. McMenahan? I'm afraid I have some bad news."

11

José opens his eyes to blinding white light. Slowly, the white gives way and he makes out a blurry figure standing over him.

"He's waking up!"

"Leroy?"

"Hang in there, buddy, you're gonna be alright."

The doctor rushes in and Leroy steps aside to let her run some tests. Bit by bit, José regains his lucidity and remembers what happened.

"Did… did we win?"

Leroy raises an eyebrow. "Now who's we here?"

"I—"

"Ah, I'm just teasing you. We all won!"

"You met the workers' demands?"

"Of course! I had no idea they were working in such horrible conditions!" he says, tugging at his shirt collar. Truth is, he would have been a lot tougher on 'em if José hadn't got shot.

"Good, that's good…" José's relieved. If he's going to die in this hospital, at least his mission was a success.

"Everything looks good, all things considered," says the doctor. "Let's give it another day, but you'll probably be ready to walk on out of here tomorrow morning."

"Really?"

"Sure, if you're feeling ready."

"Wow. You must be a medical genius. I owe you my life."

The doctor shrugs. "Just doing my job."

"Thank you."

"Sure." She walks out, yawning.

Leroy clears his throat. "There is some bad news, though."

José gulps. "Go ahead. I can take it."

"Your girlfriend, Renée. She's in jail right now. You really can't shoot down a helicopter without any consequences."

José sighs. "I don't know what she was thinking."

Leroy scratches the back of his neck. "It ain't right what they did to you, I know. But seeing as she shot first..."

José's not impressed.

"Tell you what, there's a big party I'm going to on Friday. Why don't you come along?"

"A party?"

"Yeah, up in the hills."

"At a movie star's mansion?"

"Well I don't know about that, but I'm sure there'll be plenty of Hollywood types."

"Then I must decline. I am a poet of the people, my place is with them."

Leroy looks around. "What people? I'm the only one here."

"The Fighting Mambos are with me in spirit, they just don't fuck with hospitals due to historical—"

Leroy holds his hands up. "My apologies. I didn't mean any disrespect towards your friends. But face it, José, your poetry's been selling like flapjacks. You're practically a celebrity already!" He pulls out a black business card with an address written in gold. "Why don't you get some rest, give it a think." He tosses it on the bed.

José picks it up and looks at it. "Maybe."

Leroy holds up his hands. "Decision's all yours, amigo."

José nods. "Thanks for visiting, Leroy."

Leroy's smile flattens. "You ain't got nothing to thank me for." And with that, he walks out the door.

Soon José's released from the hospital with a clean bill of health. Before he goes home, he stops by the county jail to visit Renée. In a cold gray room, they stare at each other through teal glass, phones in their hands.

"Why'd it take you so long to come visit?"

"I was in the hospital."

"Clyde told me you got out on Sunday."

"Well Clyde was wrong. He didn't even visit me."

"You know he doesn't fuck with hospitals."

"But he visited you here? With all these cops?"

Renée folds her arms and looks away. She could have lied and told him they only talked on the phone, but José would have seen right through her.

"Is it because I didn't tell you guys I used to be a CEO?"

"Kind of! How could you not tell me something like that?"

"I'm sorry. I just wanted to fit in. I thought you guys wouldn't want me around if you knew."

"Are you kidding me? With your connections you could have been a game changer!"

"Really? Or would y'all have just worried I might be undercover?"

"No, José—"

"Then what's the next mission?"

Renée can't meet his eye.

"Come on, I want to help!"

"José… Clyde's revoked your membership."

"You don't trust me? After I got shot?"

"It wouldn't be the first time a fed—"

José slams his phone on the counter, paces the cubicle, then picks it back up. "I can't believe you."

"I'm sorry, José. Clyde has protocols—"

"Fuck Clyde's protocols! I paid with my blood for the cause and this is how y'all treat me?"

"I'm sorry."

José shakes his head. "Why'd you have to shoot down that helicopter?"

"You know why."

"You don't regret it?"

"Nope. Fuck 'em."

"What about me? What about us?"

"What about us, José? All that time together and you couldn't come clean about your past. Fuck you!" Renée starts crying.

"You don't mean that."

"It's over, José. Don't fucking visit me again."

Still crying, Renée puts the phone down, gets up, and the guard escorts her back to her cell.

"Renée! Renée!"

Seeking relief from his heartbreak, José wanders the streets of Los Angeles, drinking and smoking and reading poetry to the pigeons in the park, the homeless in the alleys, to the moon and the sun and the police officer who throws him in the drunk tank for pissing on a limo he mistook for the Important Client's. When he sobers up and gets out of jail in the morning, he walks over to the Fighting Mambos Precinct #5 to give Clyde a piece of his mind, composing an angry, precise rant to give voice to all his feelings and leave Clyde no choice but to let him back into the gang. But along the way his focus slips and he thinks of his papa, the revolutionary whose revolution betrayed him, and his mama's words, Don't be like your papa. His footsteps slow and his rage fades. What's the point? He's got other things to do with his life than fight for some cause with people who don't really care about him. But is that even true? Clyde does have his protocols after all, does José really think Clyde's heart didn't break when he had to kick him out? José's rage flares up again. Who cares? Time for another drink. And if he's going to drink, he might as well drink with friends. He steps into a phone booth and gives Leroy a call.

"I think I'll come to that party after all."

"Great! I'll send a driver."

The limo winds its way up Mulholland Drive and the distant city glitters between the passing shrubbery and mansions. José's alone in the back, no music, just the rumbling of the engine and the wheels on the road. He's afraid they're going to crash, freaking out at every twist and turn, but in the end they pull up safely in the porte-cochère of a grand palazzo, a vast estate overlooking both valleys. He gets out. A valet closes the door behind him and the limo drives off. A snooty bald list-checker asks if he's on the list.

"My friend gave me this." José hands him the business card Leroy gave him.

The list-checker rips it in half. "Are you on the list or not?"

"I hope so. My name's José Jones."

"The poet?"

José nods, blushing.

"Hm. I read your latest collection. Cute." The list-checker flashes him a smile that sinks into pure loathing. He scans the list and to his dismay, finds José's name under Late Additions. He sighs and waves him in.

José walks deep into the mansion as fast as he politely can, terrified the list-checker will chase after him claiming it was all a mistake. He bursts into a crowded parlor and almost knocks a lady's drink from her hand, catching her wrist just in time.

"Sorry," he says, letting go.

"It's okay," she says, brushing her hair aside. Their eyes lock, then dart away from each other like clashing swords. He clears his throat.

"My name's José."

"I—I know." She still won't meet his eyes.

"You do?" He smiles and scratches the back of his head. "I guess that means you've read my poetry."

She nods. "It… changed me. You saved my life!"

José's taken aback. "Gracias señora, muchas gracias, but surely you must be exaggerating—" He trails off as tears fall from her eyes. He pulls out a monogrammed handkerchief, but she turns and runs away.

"Wait!" he cries, but she's already lost in the crowd. "I didn't get your name…"

"Well, well, well! Ain't that something!" Leroy claps him on the back. "Finding trouble already, I see."

"Who is that woman? She said my poetry saved her life."

"Oh she did, did she?" Leroy winks. "I wonder what her husband would have to say about that?"

"Her husband?"

"You remember our old Important Client, don't you?"

"Of course." José's face grows dark and serious. "No wonder her life needed saving."

Leroy guffaws. "Well now, that's a bit harsh, don't you think? Eliza's got all the money in the world at her fingertips! Whatever she wants, her husband's willing to pay."

"Money isn't everything, you know."

"That's just what people who grew up rich say."

"I didn't grow up rich."

Leroy thinks about that one. "Well, poets too, I guess. You know I respect the hell out of you, José, but I'll never understand the poetry business. Still, you seem to be doing pretty well for yourself, and that's a whole lot more than most poets can say. It took guts leaving our company the way you did, after all the success we'd had, and all our projected growth. It took heart."

"Thanks Leroy, but in fact it took nothing. God simply demanded it of me." José gazes up as if God's crouching on the roof, about to crash the party through the skylight.

"Well amen to that, partner. Let's get some drinks!"

Outside, the music's bumping and the stars are bright in the night sky and around the yard, dancing and mingling on the grass, lounging in deck chairs and splashing about the pool. A naked woman cannonballs off the diving board and a man in a tuxedo holds his elegant date's hair back as she vomits into a bush. Waiters cruise through the crowd carrying platters of hors d'oeuvres, and clouds of cigarette smoke form and disappear like ghosts freed at last from their earthly attachments.

José and Leroy push through to the open bar and order a couple fancy cocktails they'd never spring for if the tab was on them. A bartender whips them up in no time and hands them over with the speed, precision, and steady hand of a blindfolded sniper assembling a high powered rifle out of a bunch of junk in his garage.

The drinks are perfect but it's way too crowded. José and Leroy weave their way around the pool, searching for an empty spot in the grass. The DJ throws another song on top of the one that's already playing and it somehow works. The crowd goes wild and our heroic duo barely make it through without spilling. Giving up on the grass, José and Leroy settle for an opening at the edge of the pool. Finally able to enjoy his perfect drink, José gazes across the water at a particularly smoky gathering and his heart skips a beat. Perhaps it's his chivalrous nature, perhaps it's love at second sight, but when he sees Eliza's sullen face, listening without comment to the brash conversation of her boisterous companions, the Important Client's arm wrapped around her waist, José is filled with the resolve to reintroduce himself, to show her at least a glimpse of the poetic life, to prove to her that there's a way out of her gilded cage, that she's worth more than all the money in the world and deserves better than to waste her life trapped as a trophy and plaything of the Important Client, that despicable, disgraceful, disgusting pig. He can feel it in his soul, this is destiny!

Leroy glances over at him. José's gripping his drink so tight his hand's turned white.

"You alright, buddy?"

"How long have they been married?"

Leroy smirks. "Still got your eye on Eliza, huh? Listen, I ain't one to stand in the way of another man's passion, but you might want to brush up on the Ten Commandments. They're there for a reason, you know."

"The commandment of love is a direct order from God himself! It supersedes all of them!"

"Hmm. I've never heard that one, but I was just offering a suggestion. Anyhow, they've been married going on five years now. She's his fifth wife, you know."

"Then it won't be hard for him to find a sixth."

Leroy laughs so hard he damn near spills his drink. "I admire your confidence, buddy, I really do. But don't get ahead of yourself. All you've done so far is bump into her."

"And touched her heart with my poetry!"

Leroy scratches his chin. "Alright, maybe you got a point there. But you gotta understand something about high society. Love ain't straightforward here like it is out in the desert. It's all tied up with money, status, and reputation. You charge straight at her like a bull out the gates, these people will ruin you, and I mean *ruin*. I heard about your fiasco with one of them poets, Pete whatshisname."

"Pete… I actually don't know either."

"Well you managed to bounce back there, but you almost got yourself banned from every open mic in LA. Now imagine that but it's the whole country. And all your publishing deals fall through. And everywhere you go, you gotta look over your shoulder, just in case. Ain't no bouncing back, neither, I promise you. Is that what you want for your life?"

"No, but if God wills it—"

"Forget about God for a minute. I ain't saying there's no way to do this thing, you just gotta be strategic. Keep your hand to yourself til the river and make some friends before you sail on down. You catch my drift?"

"I think so," he says, dimly aware Leroy's making some kind of poker analogy.

"Good. Now you see that fat guy over there? Same group as Eliza, he's wearing a flower and a beret."

José squints and Leroy takes him by the shoulders and points the guy out.

"Ah si, I see him."

"That's Leon Primrose. He's a big time movie director and one of the people I invited you here to meet. I've had a handful of conversations with him and he's a big fan of your poetry. Hell, he's the reason I even heard about that whole episode with Pete. Anyhow, he ain't said anything outright, but I know how to read between the lines and I can tell he's interested in making a movie based on your latest collection."

"A movie? But that wouldn't make any sense at all! There's no plot, there's no—"

"Hey, take it up with him. Or actually, don't. If I were you, I'd let him make his movie. You get nice and entangled with him and his crowd, soon enough you'll have plenty of backup to make your move on Eliza. Having a movie made about your poems is bound to impress her, and by then, even if the Important Client wants to come after you, he'll have to contend with Leon and whoever else y'all rope into this thing."

"But what if the movie isn't good?"

"Who cares? Look, this is a win-win situation. If the movie's terrible, everyone'll say Oh, don't watch the movie, go buy the book. And if it's good, they'll probably go buy the book anyways."

"I don't know... my reputation at the open mics... they'll think I'm a sellout!"

"The hell they will! Sure, losers like Pete might spit some venom, but once it's out, if you're still pumping out poems and they're still coming straight from your heart, the people will know. The people will listen. And if they don't, well, I reckon you know better than anyone that fame and fortune ain't exactly what you're in the poetry game for."

José nods. He's really getting the picture now. "You're right. I've become too attached to my prestige. If I'm not willing to risk it all for love, my poetry is bound to suffer anyways. Thank you, Leroy." He gives him a firm hug and Leroy pats him on the back.

"That's the spirit! Now come on!" Leroy leads him around the pool, strategically approaching the group from behind the Important Client. As they near, they find Leon deep in some long winded story, but when he spots Leroy alongside LA's hottest poet, his eyes light up and he abandons his chronicle.

"Leroy! Oh dear Leroy, how are you? And can it be? Do my eyes deceive me? Are you not the great, spectacular, inimitable José Jones?"

"Yes, sir," says José.

Leon nearly faints. "Oh my days! I can hardly believe it! Come, boy, let me embrace you!"

José awkwardly steps forward and Leon kisses him on each cheek and squeezes him tight, inhaling his musky poetic scent with all his might.

Leroy chuckles. "Glad to see you haven't lost your zest for life, Leon."

"Heavens, no!" he says, releasing the poet. He gives Leroy kisses as well and shakes both his hands. "It's been too long, my friend. Please, join us." He ushers them into the group and introduces them to everyone. This time Eliza meets José's eye and smiles as she gives her name. He kisses her hand as the Important Client shakes Leroy's, and the Important Client snorts when he shakes José's.

"We've met before," he says to the group. "Many times, in fact. José was once quite the business man!"

José can tell he doesn't really mean it, but hangs onto his smile.

"Oh really?" says Leon.

"Yessiree," says Leroy, putting his arm around José's shoulder. "We were once equal partners in Saguaro Sombrero Solutions Unlimited."

"*Really?* How fascinating, I had absolutely no idea! I must confess I'm an enormous fan of your poetry, José, but what in God's name possessed you to leave such a successful venture?"

"My heart."

90

The entire clique of Hollywood élites bursts into laughter, but Leon is simply enthralled.

"Ignore them, José. They may have stakes in all the big movies, they may even know how to pick the winners, but they know nothing of art itself! You should be proud, sir, proud for staring death in the face and choosing love, for seeing through the façade of wealth and—"

"Here he goes again," says a woman in a sparkling emerald dress, rolling her eyes and smoking a cigarette from a golden holder.

"Please Leon, don't look down on us," says the tuxedoed man with his arm wrapped around her. "Wealth is all we have in life!"

The group bursts into laughter again, Leon included.

"Ah yes, my apologies. I'll save my artistic diatribes for later. Here," he says, handing José his personal card. "Do not hesitate to call on me, night or day. If I'm not home or at the phone, well, so be it, but we simply must get together sometime. We have so much to talk about!"

"I'll be sure to call."

The conversation moves on to business, some of which Leroy is able to chime in on, but it's all taking place at a higher economic altitude than even he's accustomed to. José tries to meet Eliza's eyes again and again, but each time he succeeds she looks away, pretending to be absorbed in the discussion. Still, Leon's exuberance had some effect on her, and José already feels that his mingling has paid off.

With perfect timing, during an appropriate crescendo in the conversation, Leroy and José retreat under the pretext of getting another drink. When they get to the bar, Leroy runs into another business acquaintance, and José finds himself alone, out-competed for the bartender's attention until Eliza slides up next to him and the bartender comes right over.

"I'll have what he's having," she says.

"And what'll that be?"

"The same as before," says José.

The bartender frowns. "What, am I supposed to remember you or something?"

"Sorry, I'll have—"

The bartender bursts out laughing. "I'm just fucking with you, man. Of course I remember what you got." He goes off and makes it.

Eliza brushes aside a strand of hair. "I'm sorry I ran away earlier."

"It's okay. I understand."

She raises an eyebrow.

The bartender returns with their drinks. They clink and drink up.

"I hope I'll see you around, José."

"I'm sure you will."

She smiles, then slips through the crowd like an eel through a coral reef.

"Don't think I didn't catch that," says Leroy, slapping José on the back. "You're doing well, amigo. Just get that movie going."

But José doesn't hear him, doesn't hear the crowd and the music, just her footsteps as she takes the Important Client by the arm and walks away.

12

Palm trees and statues of roaring lions line the smooth driveway to Leon's mansion. At the end, in the center of the roundabout, is a grand fountain ringed with naked cherubs, water streaming from their penises, colliding midair in a spectacular clash. Trimmed hedges grace the vast lawn; graceful ballerinas and laughing jesters, curious giraffes and wise elephants. José walks up the marble steps to the towering red double doors and rings the doorbell, smooth black rubber nested in an elaborate gold encasement. Church bells ring, and after a short moment a butler opens the left door.

"Yes?"

"My name is José Jones, I called earlier. Leon invited me over to discuss some business."

"Ah," says the butler, a mischievous smile spreading across his lips. "You're the poet."

"Yes, sir."

"No need for formalities. Please, call me Smedley." Smedley opens the door wider and José steps inside. Smedley closes it behind him and a resounding boom echoes throughout the foyer. Their footsteps clack on the checkerboard tiles as they pass beneath chandeliers and round the room's centerpiece, a marble statue of Adonis, ten feet tall with curly hair, bulging abdominals, and tasteful genitalia, his famous name etched in bold lettering upon a brass plaque at his muscular feet.

"I'm afraid Mr. Primrose isn't here at the moment. However, he's scheduled to return within the hour and has provided me with instructions in the event of your arrival."

Smedley leads him down the hall into the dining room. Ornate windows looking out to the backyard surround the handcrafted oak table and its sixteen chairs. The table is set for one. Smedley pulls out the chair and José takes a seat.

"Our chef will be with you shortly." He bows and leaves the room before José can work up the courage to tell him he just ate lunch. Twiddling his thumbs, he looks out at the yard. Sure enough, there are many more hedge sculptures—clowns, children, an octopus, a double helix, and strangely enough, a bowling ball and several bowling pins. Moments later the chef arrives, a fat, cheery woman with golden locks dressed in full white chef's attire, hat and all.

"You must be José," she beams.

"Si," he says, his voice barely escaping his throat.

"Well it's very nice to meet you. I'm Marlene, I do all the cooking around here. I have a feeling we'll come to know each other quite well, so I'd like to make a good first impression. What're you thinking?"

"Smedley left before I had a chance to tell him, but I just ate lunch before I—"

"Uh, uh, uh! If you didn't tell him, that means you want to eat!" She winks as if to say Don't worry about your diet, honey, nobody's gonna bust you for cheating!

"But I'm pretty full—"

"Then I'll whip you up something small. How about tea and crumpets?"

"Okay."

"There we go! I'll be back in a jiffy." She bustles back into the kitchen and José spreads his napkin across his lap. Behind him, the dining room continues into a sitting area complete with luxury sofas and armchairs, a massive oriental rug, two coffee tables, shelves filled with all manner of books, a fireplace, and what must be a three hundred inch television. The room is spacious, but it would still be a cozy place to snuggle up and read if the Hollywood Hills ever got any snow.

Marlene returns carrying a tray stacked with a dozen crumpets, a pot of boiling water, an assortment of teas, and a teacup. She sets it down on the table.

"Enjoy!" She giggles and scurries away.

José breaks out in a nervous sweat. Is he really supposed to eat all these? He told her twice, he just ate! Well, there's nothing to be done. Sure, in theory he could leave as many crumpets on his plate as he wants, but that would go against everything his mama taught him, against the dictums of his soul, aching for all the starving children of the world. He forces himself to burp, readies his fork and knife, and gets focused. The clock ticks. The wind blows waves through the lawn. He attacks the stack.

Half an hour later he's delirious and ready to burst. Only two crumpets remain but to finish them would require a level of fortitude he does not possess. Searching for strength, José is relieved to hear the front door open and footsteps echo down the hall. Leon walks in.

"José!"

"H–Hey Leon." Carefully, José lifts himself from his chair.

"I'm so glad you could make it!" Leon embraces him and gives him some hearty slaps on the back. José nearly vomits.

"Having some tea and crumpets, I see! Excellent choice! Mind if I have one?"

"Si," he croaks. "I mean, no, I don't mind. You can have both if you want."

"Yes, no—isn't it funny how it always means yes!" Leon laughs, spreads a glob of butter across a crumpet and eats half of it in one chomp. He smacks his lips as it travels down his throat, bulging through his skin. "An old favorite. Reminds me of my youth."

"Back in England?"

Leon smiles. "Hong Kong. But close enough." He sucks down the rest of his crumpet and eyes the other.

José belches. "Please, take it. I've already had ten."

"Ten! Well, well, I'd never have taken you to be such a lover of crumpets! I think we're going to get along quite well indeed." He snatches the other crumpet from José's plate and slurps it down whole. "Come now, and bring your tea if you like. We have much to discuss!"

Hours go by in the den with José sprawled across the divan, digesting his food while Leon paces the room praising *Poems About You, My Love* and José's live performances, from the earliest open mics to his more recent appearances at concert halls across California, many of which Leon attended incognito, due to his fame. In recounting his devious disguises, Leon sprinkles in dashes of his own life's story, then unscrews the cap and dumps out the whole bottle. José is awed and entranced. The things this man has seen, the places he's been, the people he's met. His tale is spectacular, unbelievable, wilder than any movie—longer too. The sun sets and Leon flips on a light.

"Oh dear, I hope I haven't kept you from anything," he says, knowing full well he hasn't.

"No, no," says José. "Please, keep going."

"Glad to hear it, because it's time I came clean. You see, I get rather chatty when I'm nervous, tend to meander about a bit to prolong, well, getting to the point, so to speak. So enough about me. It's time I tell it to you straight. I like your poems, José. And I like your spirit. I want to make a movie, a

96

new kind of movie, one that can compete with the Russians. Oh yes, this might be Hollywood, but you'd be surprised. You see, I believe the Russians have positioned themselves at the bleeding edge of poetic cinema. Don't ask me why, I have a million theories, but in the end, maybe they just got lucky. I don't care. All I know for certain is we're falling behind. You're a citizen, right?"

"Si, si!" he says, nodding vigorously, sweating bullets.

"Good. Then you understand the gravity of the situation." Leon stops pacing and gazes out the window. "What I'm about to ask you is a matter not only of artistic success, but American success. Will you, José Jones, join forces with me to adapt *Poems About You, My Love* to the silver screen?" He turns around and looks at José with an intense gaze fluctuating between that of a general pitching a top secret mission to an élite commando, and a lost puppy begging for food.

Though he came here anticipating this exact offer, José hesitates. He wrote his poems to describe the inner machinations of his heart, the secret currents flowing within. As far as he can tell, it makes absolutely no sense to adapt his collection to the screen. But when he thinks of Eliza, he knows what he has to do.

"It will be a challenge, but I think we can do it."

"Splendid! Absolutely wonderful!" Leon opens a cabinet and takes out champagne and two glasses. He pops the bottle, nearly shooting José in the head with the cork, and pours them each a glass. "A toast between partners in crime! To the bright future, and our new enterprise!" They clink glasses and drink up.

Three months later, they've secured financial backing and have almost finished the script. José's living in one of Leon's guest rooms, having been persuaded to move into the mansion so that they might achieve "maximal creative synchronicity." From a purely artistic standpoint, Leon's reasoning was ironclad, and José naively accepted his offer without a second thought. The writing of the film has gone very well, there's no doubt about that. José has truly grown as an artist, forced to wrangle untamed metaphysical abstractions into concrete images and sounds, people and places and stories, all woven together into a coherent whole while preserving the passion, flavor, zest, and atmosphere of the original poems. By now, José's seen some of the finest offerings of poetic cinema, not just of Russia but of the entire world, and is cautiously optimistic that his film will earn at least a modest place among them.

But not all is going well.

Every other night, as part of José's cinematic education, Leon hosts a private screening in his home theater, a tasteful, lavish, almost sacred construction dating back to Hollywood's golden age. He lets José choose whichever seat he likes and sits somewhere in the back row to avoid coloring José's impression with his uncontainable reactions and opinions, though José can still hear him chatter away through each film. But screening by screening, Leon moves forward a row, then another, then another until he's a couple rows behind José during *Vorrei Avere uno Specchio Così Potrei Guardarmi* by Andre Tarvoccio. Leon's reactions are loud and superfluous and he injects a smattering of jokes into the dialogue, jokes which would surely offend the director and which greatly embarrass José, who, with ten minutes left in the film, finally works up the courage to shush his benefactor. Apologizing profusely, Leon scurries away and for the first time, neither of them discuss the film after its conclusion. Another screening goes by without incident, but at the next one, during a particularly chilling moment of *L'amour Secret qui L'autre Mec ne Connaissait pas* by Michel Gastreaux, Leon begins creeping down the aisle. On screen, a woman walks down an empty street at night, her shadow cast on the wall, stalked by another shadow wielding a knife, the owner of which can't be seen. José nearly jumps out of his seat when he feels a pair of cold, sweaty hands massaging his neck.

"Leon! What are you doing?"

Leon giggles. "You looked so tense I thought you might like a massage."

"Of course I'm tense! This is a scary movie!"

Leon bows, still giggling. "My apologies. I simply… couldn't resist." He tiptoes away through the seats and leaves the theater. José tries to keep watching the movie, but now he's also afraid of being snuck up on again. After a couple more minutes of pure terror, clinging to his arm rests like a cat to a tree branch, for the first time during his stay, José abandons a film midway through.

Normally Smedley arrives during the credits to bus his popcorn bowl back to the kitchen, but since he's nowhere to be seen, José takes it upon himself. When he walks in, he finds Marlene washing pots and pans and smoking a cigarette. He places the bowl with the rest of the dirty dishes and catches her by surprise.

"José!" She quickly ashes her cigarette in the sink, then notices the bowl. "You didn't have to do that—just leave it on the rack outside next time."

"It's no problem at all, I can—"

"Leave it outside!" She turns back to her dishes and starts scrubbing furiously. José turns to go, then she drops the pan and sighs. "I'm sorry, José, I didn't mean to snap at you."

"It's alright, Marlene—"

"No, it's not. Listen, about my smoking in here. Would you mind keeping that between us?"

José shrugs. "Sure."

"Thanks. Leon doesn't like me smoking near the food, even after I'm done cooking, but everything would take a lot longer if I went outside for every cigarette."

"But Leon smokes, even indoors."

"I know. He didn't always care, and he never comes in here anyways, but still... sometimes he gets mad and starts making rules, and once he makes a rule, no matter how drunk he was, you've gotta follow it. The man grew up playing cricket, understand?"

"I understood until you said that."

"No strikes. The ball hits the wicket and you're off the pitch." She laughs and gets back to scrubbing.

José decides to read in the living room and finds Leon already there reading something old and leather bound, a glass of fine liquor rolling around in his hand. He walks softly to the bookshelf and selects *tales from yonder deep*, a book of experimental cyber-nautical poems, if you can call them that. He sits across from Leon, far away in an armchair by the TV, and flips past the introduction. He's immediately engrossed. The fragments floating before his eyes strike him less as poems than bubbles of thought, the start and end often omitted, pure glimpses into the primordial flow of consciousness, free from context, from structure, from—

"You didn't finish the movie," says Leon without looking up from his book.

"It... wasn't for me."

Leon tuts at him. "One must not shy away from the horrors of life."

José looks around, thinks about it. "But isn't that the point of living in a house?"

Leon blows a laugh out his nose, then closes his book in one hand. "That's what I like about you, José, you keep me on my toes. Makes me feel fresh and young, like I still have some growing up to do."

"Everyone has room to grow, Leon."

"For a man my age, there's only one thing left with room to grow."

José gulps, eyeing the bulge in Leon's trousers. "What's that?"

Leon chortles with gusto and might, his kingly stomach heaving as his mirth bellows out. "Oh, sweet, kind, innocent José. There's no need to beat off around the bush. I'm referring to my weight, of course. And my wealth, I suppose, but wealth is a sort of weight in its own way, as are reputation, status, all the tangible intangibles one can spend one's whole life pursuing, amassing, conserving. But in the end it all comes from hunger of a sort, and therefore it's all weight to me. You'll understand someday when you're old. Perhaps you already do."

José scratches his head. "You could always go on a diet."

"Oh, yes, I've tried, believe me. Yet in the end, I always order Marlene to help me surrender to gluttony and sloth!"

"You could ask her not to listen to you."

"I have. But when push comes to shove, I'm very persuasive!" Leon chuckles and finishes his drink. "I think I'll pour myself another glass. Would you like one?"

José finds himself lying on the couch in the den. Save for the moon shining through the window, the room is completely dark. Something's perched across his scalp, a cold, wrinkly hand sliding through his hair, massaging his skull.

"Sweet, kind, innocent José..." Leon whispers.

José tries to speak but he can't move his lips. He lets out a grunt. Leon stops massaging.

"Ah... you're awake I see... let me, um, fetch you some water." He withdraws from the room. "Didn't put enough..."

José groans as he regains control of his arms. His legs are prickly but he lifts them over the side and stands up. He shakes his head and flubbers his lips, then waddles out the door. The light hurts his eyes. He hears Leon coming up the stairs and ducks into another room, quietly closing the door just before Leon reaches the top. Leon passes by and enters the den.

"José?"

His ear to the door, José holds his breath.

Leon chuckles. "José, where are you? José?"

José hears him walk past, then exhales when he's gone. He slowly opens the door, looks both ways, then tiptoes to his room. He locks the door behind him and breaks out in chills. He's shaking so badly he lets himself fall onto the bed. He rolls around, wrapping himself in blankets like a churro in a tortilla. He's never eaten that before in his life, but now he wishes he could eat a hundred of them. Then he imagines himself taking a bite and hearing their screams. He pulls the covers over his head and squeezes his eyes shut. Think of something else think of something else—he can't remember anything from... he woke up and... there was the drink...

José shakes his head. He can't think it. If he thinks it then it's real. But for a poet of his caliber, no amount of pretending can keep the truth from shining through. Dark clouds part and words form in the swirling light. He raped you he raped you he tried to rape you did he rape you?

José sits up clutching his head and opens his eyes. He clenches his asshole. Then sticks his hand down his pants. He lets out a huge breath that relaxes his entire body, then takes a few more deep ones. He wasn't raped, but he almost might as well have been. He goes into the bathroom and kneels before the toilet, ready to throw up but unable to. He looks at himself in the still water. Is this what it takes to make a movie? Is this the life his mama wanted for him? It all comes gushing out.

13

The next day, José refuses to leave his room. He tells Smedley he's sick and asks him to keep Leon away, a request at which Smedley doesn't bat an eye. All morning he agonizes over what to do. By all means he should get the hell out of there, but the screenplay's almost finished and more importantly, they're having dinner with a number of Leon's associates tomorrow night, including Eliza and the Important Client. Is there a way he can back out and preserve his reputation? Try as he might, he can't think of one. He hasn't built up enough rapport with Eliza yet, and with the movie still unfinished, Leon could tear him to shreds. Why does it have to be this way? Why are there people like Leon?

He gets out of bed and opens the curtains, filling the room with light. If he's going to be stuck in here all day, he might as well write. He takes a shower, then rings for Smedley and asks for a doubleshot espresso.

"Feeling better, I see."

"No, I'd just like an espresso."

Smedley gives him an understanding nod, then leaves.

For the first hour, José can't get a single word out, but he refuses to take his eyes off the page. Then, suddenly, as a lone cloud passes over the sun, a flood of images bursts forth from within, emotional scenes and impactful dialogue, crucial and unexpected details, moments of pause and reflection, insights into the characters' inner beings, all assaulting him with such force and speed that he spends the rest of the day in a frenzy, his survival instincts and creative impulses perfectly aligned. The sooner he finishes the script, the sooner this nightmare can end.

At three in the morning, his mind is still flooded with ideas, but his swollen fingers lack the strength to type. He goes to bed and turns off the light. As he lays in the darkness, his mind swimming, he realizes Leon never tried to visit him today. He turns the light back on and gets up, checks the lock on the door, and goes back to bed.

He wakes up around eight in the morning but isn't tired. He's still getting plenty of ideas and writes for an hour, then decides he'd better keep up appearances around the house so he can bring his A-game to dinner. His hand trembling, he unlocks the door and makes his way to the dining room. Leon's already there, eating a hearty breakfast of eggs, sausages, crumpets, cantaloupe, and coffee.

"Ah, José! Feeling better?"

"Si," he croaks, sitting opposite him. Marlene appears and asks if he'd like some breakfast. José says he'll have what Leon's having and she tells him it's coming right up. Leon keeps eating and José stays silent, listening to the sounds of fork and knife on plate, food between teeth, liquid slurped, birds chirping in the backyard. He pours himself a glass of water so he has something to do.

"We don't have to work on the film today if you're not feeling up to it," says Leon between bites.

"No, I can work. I actually wrote a lot yesterday."

"Oh really?"

"Sometimes I receive my greatest inspiration during illness."

"Hm." Leon nods and eats, thinking about it. "Yes, I suppose illness can shake us out of our daily modes of thinking… quite interesting."

José's on the verge of confronting him, but something in him says wait, your time will come. Marlene arrives with his food and he scarfs it down.

Later in the den, José walks Leon through the new additions he's made. Leon's comments are all positive, but the excitement isn't there anymore, he's just going through the motions. When it's time to start putting new ideas down on the page, José finds he's doing all the work. Leon keeps yawning and pacing the room, checking his watch and looking out the window before finally excusing himself to ensure his staff's dinner preparations are up to snuff. Left alone, José searches every cabinet and drawer for whatever he was drugged with, but can't find it. He does, however, find a photo album with "Les Garçons" written on a piece of tape stuck to the front. He opens it and finds dozens of pictures, all of Leon with his arm around a tall, skinny boy out back in the hedge sculpture garden. Handwritten beneath each picture: Leon + William, Leon + Francisco, Leon + Albert, etc. They're probably all over eighteen, but next to Leon one can't help but view them as children. José shudders as he turns the pages, watching the hedge sculptures multiply with each photo, then finds himself in there, the last garçon in the album. Innocent enough at the time, the image has taken on a sinister quality, José's naivete on full display next to Leon's feigned friendliness, his predatory calculations grinding away beneath the mask.

He puts the album away and gets back to writing, now desperate to finish before Leon changes his mind about the whole project.

At seven thirty, Smedley knocks on the open door to inform José that the first guests have arrived. José thanks him, finishes typing what he's in the middle of, then heads downstairs to the formal dining room, an entirely separate affair from the table he's eaten most of his meals at. With red wallpaper and portraits of Primroses past, candles in brass holders along the walls and in the chandelier, maroon carpeting, and a mahogany dinner table with twenty-four seats, the formal dining room evokes a decidedly regal, almost medieval atmosphere apart from the electric ceiling lights. It's obvious why Leon prefers to host his more high-flying guests here. To José's surprise, half the table's already seated, including Eliza and the Important Client. There aren't any open seats anywhere near her, and he curses himself for losing track of the time. He sits down and pours himself a glass of wine from the bottle on the table. He swirls it around, smells it, and when he doesn't notice anything odd, takes a sip. The guests are all enraptured by the Important Client and Leon's approving discussion of the President's latest tax cuts and deregulatory efforts. José doesn't know much about politics, but he knows the Fighting Mambos hate the President and he was always down with what they're about, so he's careful to stay out of it.

"I wish, however, that he would make a bit more of an effort to get this AIDS situation under control," says Leon.

"Oh you'd like that, wouldn't you?" The Important Client winks and the whole table laughs in good fun. Leon blushes but his sexual proclivities aren't exactly a secret among his friends, nor in Hollywood at large.

"I should hope we'd all like that. It's not just the gays it affects, you know."

"Yeah, just them and their wives!" shouts some wisecracker. The room erupts in laughter, but José doesn't find it funny at all. Right after his mama died, he'd received word that his brother, Jorge, after a lifetime in the underworld of Mexico City, had contracted AIDS and was on his deathbed. They hadn't spoken in years, but everything standing between them melted away as soon as he got the call. After trekking through the desert and hitchhiking his way south, José made it to the hospital just in time, on the day of his death. Jorge was thin as a stick and could barely move, but they spent the afternoon talking about the old days, and all of a sudden those days didn't feel so old anymore, and they laughed and cried and felt the warmth of brotherhood one last time.

He sheds a tear and dries his eyes with his napkin. A hand slaps him on the back and a jolt runs through him.

"Whoa there, didn't mean to scare you. How's it going, partner?"

"Leroy? Oh, I'm so happy to see you," he says, getting up and giving him a tight hug that does not go unnoticed by the others at the table, especially Eliza, whose heart is touched. "Leon didn't tell me you were coming."

A mere oversight, Leon wants to interject, but he's too entangled in listening to the Important Client deliver a pompous monologue about youth who don't want to work.

"Well, here I am," says Leroy, taking the seat next to José. "How's the movie coming along?"

"The script's almost there."

"What's that mean?"

"It'll be done by the end of next week if I can help it." José pretends to take a sip of his wine and whispers out of the corner of his mouth. "I've gotta get out of here."

"What?"

"You're making a movie?" asks Eliza from down the table, bringing the political discussion to a screeching halt until a man with coke-bottle glasses seizes the opportunity to impress the Important Client with his opinions on the latest South American coup.

José smiles. "Si."

"What's it about?"

José sighs and chuckles. "It's hard to explain—"

"That's no good. Not in this town."

"It's about a man's heart," says Leroy. "It's about life and love, staying true to yourself and away from the pitfalls of life. It's a journey through the soul, but also through the American Southwest, and most of all, it's about a detective. That's what I got from the book, anyhow." He gives José a wink.

José's first impulse is to laugh and correct him, but he's struck by the accuracy of Leroy's assessment. How could he not have seen it? How could he have been so blind to the clear themes running through his entire collection? Even the script, for all its additions and changes, remains remarkably faithful to Leroy's summary.

"That's still pretty vague, but I love a good mystery," says Eliza. "This movie wouldn't happen to be based on *Poems About You, My Love*, would it?"

"Ah, si, it is," says José, blushing.

"You should have just said so! That'll make a great— well, I don't want to jinx it, but I'll definitely watch it!"

"I'll send you a ticket to the premiere."

"I'd love that."

The Important Client reaches into his coat pocket and comes out empty handed. "Eliza, can I borrow your lighter?"

"What happened to yours?"

"I seem to have misplaced it."

"Oh it's somewhere in my purse, can't you just use a candle?"

The Important Client grimaces, then seizes a candle in his fist and lights his cigarillo. Eliza tries to turn back to José and Leroy, but she's swept up in a torrent of questions about her latest film from the man in the coke-bottle glasses. Leroy elbows José under the table and makes a clicking noise through his teeth. José kicks his shin and they both laugh and drink their wine.

Eventually the table is full and Smedley, Marlene, and two of her assistants arrive with the food. Once his guests are served, Leon stands and taps his glass with a knife.

"Quiet now, quiet please. Thank you. I'd like to extend my gratitude to each and every one of you for gathering here tonight. It is truly a pleasure to have my home filled with the conversation and laughter of kindred souls. Your friendship is worth more to me than all the wealth in the world. And now, a toast to my newest friend, my partner in crime and co author of our upcoming film, *Memories of You, My Love*. José, it's been a pleasure hosting you and an honor to be involved in your creative process. May our endeavors bear fruit!" He raises his glass and everyone cheers as they clink with those closest to them, all smiling with the suspicion that José is Leon's latest boy toy. José grins and bears it, but when the toast is finished his appetite is gone.

After dinner they break for dessert and digestifs in the living room. José and Leroy angle to peel Eliza away from her companions, but the Important Client has his arm firmly wrapped around her waist and soon they're cornered by Leon.

"Enjoying yourselves?"

"Yes sir," says Leroy. "You got a real nice place. Glad I finally got an invitation!"

Leon laughs and pats him on the shoulder. "You've earned it, my friend. I cannot thank you enough for introducing me to José. Our collaboration on *Memories of You, My Love* has been a revelation."

"It sure has," says José, mustering up some of the genuine joy he's felt working with Leon, stuffing his uneasiness down somewhere it doesn't quite fit.

"Well I can't wait to see it," says Leroy. "I read the book, and I thought it was pretty good, but I'm not a big poetry guy so for me, the movie's gonna be the real test. No offense, pal."

José laughs. "None taken. I'd expect no less from a world class television repairman."

"Television repair?" asks Leon. "You?"

"Yes, sir. Believe it or not, I wasn't always a CEO!"

"I could have never imagined!"

José furrows his brow. "I told you, Leon, that's how we met."

"Oh yes, yes indeed. The television mishap at the bar."

Leroy gives José a stern look, hoping he didn't dig up those bandits.

Leon slurps a pickle off a toothpick and starts choking.

José hesitates but Leroy springs into action. He squeezes the old man like a medicine ball until the pickle flies out across the room and smacks onto the Important Client's forehead. Everyone cheers and applauds. The Important Client flings the pickle aside and wipes his angry face with a nearby curtain. Eliza shoves down her laughter, knowing she'd get an earful later, but she catches José's eye and they share a smile. Yet in that moment she detects something more than just shared amusement—despair, deep and tortured, an icy chasm between José's hopes for this world and the world itself. She looks away.

"Thank you, Leroy," gasps Leon, shooting a quick glare at José as if to say You would have left me to die, wouldn't you?

"No problemo."

"I must find myself some water..." He stumbles off on wobbling legs, helped by the man in the coke bottle glasses.

Leroy checks his watch. "Smoke break? Oh, I forgot, you don't—"

"No, I could really use one today."

Leroy nods gravely and they head for the back. They try to catch Eliza's attention one more time, but she's once again trapped in the clutches of the Important Client.

The backyard is lit by orbs of light atop patina altars covered with intricate tangles of sculpted vines and flowers. Leroy is so entranced by their craftsmanship that he doesn't even notice the dozens of hedge sculptures surrounding him.

"They don't make stuff like this anymore. People who made things used to care about the people who saw it and what they'd think about it. Now... well, I ain't one to judge. Maybe they still do." Leroy pulls out a pack of cigarettes and hands one to José. He strikes a match and lights them both, then waves it out. They smoke in silence, watching it wind around the light like DNA, like clouds drifting across the full moon.

"I think Leon tried to rape me."

Leroy takes another drag, nodding slightly. "What happened?"

"He drugged me, but he didn't use enough and I woke up."

"Then he must really like you," says a voice from behind.

They turn around and see a grubby man in overalls holding an enormous pair of scissors.

112

"Who are you?" asks José.

"I'm the gardener."

"Really? How come I've never seen you?"

The gardener smiles. "I am seen when I choose to be seen. Do you think these hedges trim themselves?"

"I guess not."

"What did you mean there just now?" asks Leroy.

The gardener gazes up at the moon. "If Leon failed in his... attempt, then it was by no means an accident or a mistake."

José shakes his head. "That doesn't make any sense."

"Why do you expect people to make sense? Aren't you a poet?"

"I am," he says, his nose held high. "How did you know?"

"I've kept my eye on you. You're different from the others. You're not just here to become a victim. If you were, I'd be digging another hole for another hedge to be trimmed, perhaps, into the shape of a cactus wearing a sombrero and waving maracas."

"So he's done this to other people?" asks José, acting surprised, looking around at the hedge sculptures with a morbid suspicion that seems to be confirmed by a glint in the gardener's eye.

"Oh yes. He can't help himself."

"That's a load of shit," says Leroy, spitting in the dirt, shaking with rage. "Every man's responsible for his actions."

"I've got no quarrel with that," says the gardener. "I'm just saying what I've seen. I've seen him hesitate before, trying to resist his dark urges. But this is the first time I've seen him fail. When you've got enough money that you can keep the police away, and you don't have anyone around to stop you, and you've got big problems like Leon has—I mean deep psychological, emotional problems, horrible trauma, you know, trust me, it's bad—without the ability to heal, without a lifetime of discipline and self-control behind him, he stopped being a person so much as a vessel for dark forces to act through."

Leroy shakes his head. "I can't accept that."

"Have you ever tried to quit smoking?"

"That's different."

"Is it?"

"Sure is. I can buy a pack of cigarettes at the corner store. Takes a lot more than that to build up trust with a guy and then drug him up and, you know..." He looks to José, but tears are streaming down the poet's face. His cigarette falls to the ground and burns on without him.

"He's right, Leroy. Leon's a monster but I know him. I know who he wishes he was. I don't know how he became like this, and I won't make any excuses for him, but he's complicated."

"You've got Stockholm syndrome!" shouts Leroy.

The gardener gently shushes him.

José laughs and shakes his head and wipes away his tears. "No. Just the twisted empathy of a poet. I promise you, when this movie's done, I'll make sure this never happens to anyone else."

"That might just end you," says Leroy. He drops his cigarette and crushes it into the dirt with his boot. "But I'll hold you to it."

They grip hands and bring it on in, sealing the promise. When they pull apart, the gardener's gone.

14

THE END. José leans back in his chair and breathes a happy sigh. At long last, the screenplay is finished. He looks out at the sun-soaked gardens and basks in the moment. He still has a long road ahead of him before he's free, but this chapter is over. Leon returns from the bathroom and sees the page.

"It's done?"

José nods, grinning wide.

"Right then." Leon takes the pages from the typewriter, sits down at his desk, and starts reading.

"I'll be back."

"Mm."

José leaves and goes outside to have a smoke. He gazes at the lamp he and Leroy made their fateful pact beneath and watches a butterfly flutter by and land on a sculpted vine, perhaps mistaking it for a real flower.

When he gets back, Leon's finished reading. He's staring into space, oblivious to José's return.

"Well?"

Leon gently emerges from his reverie, blinking in blissful confusion. "José..." He trails off.

José waits.

"José, this script... won't be needing any revisions."

"Really?"

"It's perfect, José. Truly. Words cannot describe how grateful I am to have been a part of your process."

José gulps, wondering if Leon's got some kind of angle here. But despite it all, he seems sincere. "Thank you, Leon. Thanks for the opportunity—"

"Oh please, a talent like yours was bound to be recognized. I'm just glad I was the first to get my hands on you."

José nods. "Thank you."

Leon clears his throat and stands up. "Well then. I think it's time you saw the studio."

After a nauseating ride down narrow winding roads, the limo cruises out onto straight wide streets lined with palm trees and unseasonably green lawns. They pass the Beverly Hills sign and weave through traffic, already thick at two o'clock, until finally, almost out of nowhere, Big Time Studios appears. The gates open as the limo rolls up, splitting the hourglass logo in half. Leon rolls down his tinted window and waves to the smiling guard. José's eyes are wide with wonder as they pass between warehouses through all the studio bustle—extras, golf carts, workers hauling giant paintings, an elephant, clowns, caterers pushing carts of silver platters, vintage cars, pianos, a diva crying, an actor punching the wall and yelling at scared men wearing walkie talkies—this is it! This is where the magic happens!

Here in his domain, in the mystical halls of cinematic conception, Leon is revered as a King by some, a God by others. From lowly production assistants and office enablers to top studio executives, everyone they pass drops everything to suck up to him. It ain't hard to see: one false move and José could find his movie canceled and his career wiped from the face of the Earth, almost as if it never existed, kept alive only in the hearts of those he truly touched—and even they might find themselves with targets on their backs. The risks are great, but José's dreams are greater. Eliza—to leave her trapped with that evil man—his heart couldn't bear it. Not once does he entertain the possibility that she might not want to leave the Important Client, and only once does he suppose she might find her way out on her own. He knows she could do it. Her strength of spirit is clear as day. But God made him love her for a reason. Yes, it's his duty to whisk her away from her miserable life. An escape without him, while possible, while better than her current situation, would still be something different altogether. Only he can give her what he can give her. He knows that, he's never been so sure.

They reach the top floor of executive production. The secretary hangs up the phone and springs out of her chair.

"Good afternoon, Leon! Everyone's waiting in Conference Room B."

"B? I'm sorry, we're not making a B movie, Catherine. Please, tell them we'll be waiting in Conference Room A."

"But Leon—"

"Thank you!" Leon bustles down the hall. José breaks into a jog just to keep up.

"Leon, are you sure—"

"José, I know you mean well, I know you're new here, but please, don't question how I run my business."

Leon bursts into Conference Room A, interrupting an intense, important meeting between the foreign acquisition team and a group of formidable Japanese investors.

"Stop what you're doing, everyone, stop right now!"

The meeting grinds to a halt.

"We'll get back to this in a moment," he says, gesturing at the pie charts and growth projections on the screen. "What I have to share is far more important."

Despite Leon's reputation, the Japanese investors aren't amused. Yet in a just a few short minutes, Leon pulls off the impossible, winning everyone over with a powerful film pitch, alternating between English and fluent Japanese, mixing allusions to the great filmmakers and poets of history with geopolitical calculations and strong opinions on the direction of international finance. José's been around the block in business, but Leon's a true wizard. In the end the whole room gives a standing ovation, and Leon and José walk out of there with hundreds of millions in financing.

Leon claps José on the back. "Piece of cake!" He laughs and leaves a stunned José to wander after him.

And so José stays on at the mansion to avoid rocking the boat, telling himself it isn't so bad now that he's busy at the studio every day. But each night as Smedley drives him back up Mulholland Drive, his whole body tenses, his breath gets shallow, his dread grows more powerful than the night before. He works longer hours at the studio, barely eating, living off coffee and cigarettes, completely surrendered to his old ways. Just until this is over, Mama, he whispers every morning as he lights his first of the day. I promise.

Soon they start filming, and on set it becomes obvious why Leon's one of the biggest director-producer-CEOs in the business. The performances he brings out of his actors, the way he places his cameras, hides his microphones, controls his lighting, interprets parts of the script José didn't even realize were open to interpretation—the man is a true maestro. Every day José gains new insights into the grueling, deceptive, beautiful nature of cinema, into humanity itself. He almost forgets who Leon really is until the day is done and they drive back up that hill.

When filming's over and the celebrations have finished, Leon takes José aside and politely informs him that the edit is really between the editor and the director. Nevertheless, José can rest assured that he will have full authority to review the film and make any changes he wishes before the final cut. José takes the news well enough, relieved at not having to spend the next few months in a small room with Leon, but he's also anxious and frustrated that his film is being pieced together without his input. Yet everyone he talks to tells him he's been extremely lucky to have had the influence he's had on the script, on set, and especially to have final cut privileges. But that's not what he wants to hear so he continues wandering the studio grounds, complaining to whoever will listen until one day an old man hits him over the head with his walking stick.

"You spoiled brat! Do you even understand how things used to be, how hard directors fought to get the final cut?"

"No, sir, I'm sorry—"

"You better be! I worked on *Citizen Blaine*, that was the very first you know, and, and—" The old man collapses and José catches him and calls for help. His eyes roll back, his mouth froths, his body seizes up. José can feel the old man slipping away. Suddenly, he stops, his eyes roll back into place, and he smiles. "Nose blood…"

"What?"

But that's all the old man can manage before it's Fade to Black.

Opening night finally arrives. Everyone who's anyone tried to get a ticket, but there's only room for the crème de la crème of Hollywood high society. Normally there wouldn't be such large swarms of paparazzi for an arthouse flick like *Memories of You, My Love*, but Leon's larger than life reputation and José's underground open mic Fighting Mambos associating corporate rejectionist poetic credibility make for an establishment-renegade, fat-thin, bing-bang combo that proves irresistible to all. Speculative murmuring spreads through the crowd, each carrier hoping and praying that they're right so they can say they knew from the start when it all pans out—that maybe, just maybe, this will be the movie to shake Hollywood out of its addiction to safe big-budget blockbusters and thrust *real art* back into the spotlight—if it ever had it, wonder the artists in the crowd, not just the beauty rivals and clout chasers, but the *real* artists, the ones who have been through it, the ones who fight for true feelings and expression and raw truth against the suffocating influence of this increasingly corporatized world, the ones who blah blah blah, etcetera, etcetera. You know the type.

The limo pulls up at the Chinese Theater and Leon and José step out into the flashing lights. A forest of microphones scrape their cheeks and pummel their sides as they run the red gauntlet. Leon holds up his hand to preclude any questions, but José's unable to resist.

"How faithful is this film to your poetry?"

"Go see for yourself."

"Do you feel like you've compromised your integrity by translating this to the big screen?"

"Not at all!" he says, feeling a bit sick.

"Are the rumors that you're having an affair with—"

"Come along now, José," says Leon, dragging him by the arm. "There'll be plenty of time for questions after the film!"

They pass the guards and enter the lobby. The place is full of big name celebrities taking pictures with the posters and cutouts and lining up for drinks and popcorn before the show. Three of the film's main actors spot them and walk over. There's Rodolfo Ferrari who plays the unnamed protagonist, presumably a stand-in for José, Grace Jolla who plays the unnamed love interest who Rodolfo's character has memories of, and leading the way is Henry Lodz, one of Hollywood's most handsome, mysterious, iconic rising stars, who in a few short years has firmly solidified his reputation as a chameleon destined to be

120

remembered as one of the greats of the era. He plays Noel Esormirp, the third man on the side of the protagonists' love affair, watching from hidden vantage points, sometimes by chance, sometimes by his own design. Trapped in a web of desire, obsession, and loneliness, Noel is unable to reconcile his simultaneous embodiment of spider and insect, and meets a tragic end. There's no mention of any Noel character in *Poems About You, My Love*, but through steady reasoning, Leon convinced José of Noel's necessity in the film, that he's present in the poems through his implicit absence, that he even represents the reader himself, a voyeur into José's most intimate feelings. Eventually José had been persuaded, and hadn't thought much about Noel once filming began, but as the editing process carried on, he realized Noel plays a much larger part in the film than he anticipated. In fact, the night before the premiere, he re-read *Poems About You, My Love* and found the movie had strayed a lot farther from it than he'd realized. He still thinks it's good, that it still captures his innermost passions, but he's shocked at how caught up in the moment he'd become, how easily his magnum opus had faded into hazy memory.

"Leon! José!" Henry embraces them, followed by the other two.

José feels dangerously off-balance. The conversation goes in one ear and out the other even though he's speaking along just fine. Memories of Henry's charisma and gravitas on set flood into his mind and he pores over every one of Noel's scenes, searching in vain for imperfection. Soon José's almost convinced that Rudolfo and Grace and everyone else in the movie didn't even make the final cut, that Henry Lodz will stand alone up there on the silver screen. He decides he shouldn't drink tonight, then excuses himself and gets in line at the bar.

"José! José!" Finally he hears her. Eliza's waving at him. He waves her over and when the people around him start to grumble he puts them in their place declaring that he's José Jones and they're lucky he doesn't cut straight to the front of the line.

"Yeesh, sorry about that," she says when the commotion's died down.

"Don't be. These people have no respect for line cutting etiquette." He looks around and doesn't see the Important Client and relaxes a little. "I'm glad you could make it."

"I wouldn't miss it for the world. Besides, I received an invitation from the writer himself."

José blushes. "I didn't expect this movie to get so much attention."

"Well you should have. You're working with Leon, after all."

He nods, looking a bit grim.

"He sent us tickets, too, by the way."

"I… didn't know that. Though I guess I should have." Over her shoulder he spots Leroy crossing the lobby with a bucket of popcorn. Leroy grins and salutes him and enters the theater.

Eliza laughs. "Don't worry, I'm using the one you sent me. I can't stand watching movies with my husband. He just sits there nitpicking every little detail and it's impossible to follow anything."

Something warm bubbles up inside. Before José can respond, it's their turn to order.

Drinks and popcorn in hand, they enter the theater. As they walk down the aisle, whispers and glances shimmer in their wake. When they take their seats, optimally selected to be as close to the screen as possible without having to crane their necks, nobody has any doubt about what's going on between them—just for how long. Some claim to have known for months, others since the most recent party at Leon's, and a few even claim it came to them in a dream that very morning, a premonition from God himself, or whoever it is that runs the projector every night. But the truth is, José and Eliza are on their first date. In the back row, Leon tries to keep the Important Client engrossed in gossip about secret financial dealings while keeping a jealous eye on his poet protegé. The Important Client's no fool, though. He's seduced the wives of many a cuckold in his time, and he can smell an affair from a mile away.

"I'm getting chills," says Eliza. "I've never watched a movie with the guy who wrote it before."

"Then I'd better hope it's good!"

"Oh, you know it's good."

José shakes his head. "My opinion doesn't matter. The audience decides."

"If you thought it was bad, you wouldn't have invited me to sit next to you."

"Maybe. Or maybe the movie's not the point." He slides his arm around her shoulders and she leans into him as the lights dim and the curtains part. The spotlight shines on Ricky Poppins, the short, dapper host. He's wearing a black suit and sporting a brown crew cut that might look military if he wasn't such a teddy bear. As usual, most of the crowd fawns over this adorable man while the rest grow impatient.

"Hey everyone! Wow. Full house tonight!"

Laughs.

"I could just kiss you all! I saw the test screening earlier and—wow. I'll tell ya, I sure shed some tears. My heart was touched, but it's not what you think, and I don't know how I feel about that. You know, earlier today I'd been thinking about—"

"Play the movie!"

The unadoring minority boos.

"Hm." For a second, cold pomposity slips across Ricky's face, but just for a second. "Alright, the crowd has spoken! Without further ado, Big Time Studios presents: *Memories of You, My Love.*"

The spotlight dims and Ricky hurries offstage. The whole crowd applauds with whoops and whistles until the famous animation of a giant hourglass towering over skyscrapers appears on the screen.

Within the first few minutes, the realization that's been looming over José finally crashes down. This film has been stolen from him, right under his nose. He can't believe he didn't see it. From the very beginning, starting at Leon's acquiescence to leaving the protagonist lovers unnamed as they were in the book, the seeds were planted for the usurpation of his artistic vision. Every question Leon asked, every suggestion he made was an opportunity seized to sneak his own story in. José thinks back in horror to the day he approved the final cut, so eager to leave the cramped editing room and get away from Leon that he completely missed what was right in front of him. Yes, perhaps upon the first, maybe even the second and third viewings, the audience will believe as José did that the lovers are the protagonists, that *Memories of You, My Love* is their story. But, as Henry Lodz must have known full well when he accepted the part, the real protagonist is Noel Esormirp, the conniving voyeur so carefully placed, so skillfully played, that the observant viewer feels his hidden presence in every scene—even those he's not in. José finishes his drink and curses himself for not having bought two, or three, or a whole bottle. He's so enraged that he almost forgets who's in his arms, enthralled by every frame passing before her eyes.

124

During the pivotal scene where the lovers discover each other's affection, José is faced with a daunting decision. Should he go in for a kiss, or is Eliza enjoying the movie so much that his kiss would get in the way? Sweating bullets, his eyes darting between the unnamed lovers as if they each represented a choice, he doesn't even notice Eliza raising her lips to his and making contact. At long last they show each other how they really feel, losing themselves in the heat of their passion, jostling the people seated near them and ignoring their protests. The Important Client notices the commotion and when the screen flashes white during a scene in the snow, he sees who's causing it.

"So that's who it is," he mutters, grinding his cigarillo in his teeth.

When the film's over, it receives a standing ovation. The audience can't believe it—the dawn of a new movement in American cinema is here, today, brought into being by *Memories of You, My Love*. Leon, José, and the stars are compelled to come up before the screen and take a bow. José gives Leon a cold glance that says I know what you did, but Leon simply maintains his smile. José catches sight of the Important Client in the back talking on his cellphone and his stomach goes cold. Ricky reappears, microphone in hand.

"Wow! What a tour de force! Let's have another round of applause for the people who made it happen!"

The audience explodes into an unruly show of gratitude and ecstasy. So many of them are barely lucid, lost in a torrent of memories and sudden insights, glowing with warmth as their mental and emotional wounds finally begin to heal. One veteran even cries out in astonishment as his amputated leg starts growing back. Ricky gives Leon the microphone.

"What would you like me to do with this?" he asks, garnering some laughter. "I suppose first and foremost I should thank my cast, my crew, everyone involved in making this film. We have exceeded my wildest expectations. And most of all I should thank José Jones for his help writing the screenplay and of course for his excellent book *Poems About You, My Love*, without which none of this would have been possible. Please, I know you've all just seen the movie, but I cannot stress enough what a revelation his poetry has been for me. Go read the book!"

More laughter, though one or two are thinking about it.

"Now I could spend quite some time speaking about what this film means to me and how we've drawn a line in the sand and stood our ground, refusing at last to let the Russians take poetic cinema without a fight, but I'll save that for my talk show appearances and let the man from whose mind this vision sprung speak for himself—come on over, José!"

The crowd roars and José accepts the mic from Leon and wipes it off on his pants.

"Thank you, Leon. Working with you has been a unique opportunity. I never in my life thought I would get to make a feature film, let alone one based on my poetry. These poems came from my heart, and at first, I did not see their cinematic potential. But you helped me realize that potential buried deep within them, and this film is the result of our excavation."

In the back, big tough goons with sunglasses and earpieces block the exits. José turns pale. Leroy notices, then makes a discreet call on his cellphone.

"I... have some pressing business to attend to, so I cannot speak for long. However, I will leave you with this. Someday, close readers of *Poems About You, My Love* will

126

come to understand that this film contains not only my life's story, but Leon's."

Now it's Leon's turn to go pale.

"At first I was upset that he snuck it in without asking me, right under my nose. But in the end, it was my own fault for not noticing. Besides, how can such things be avoided in creative collaboration, in adaptation? No, I'm at peace with it now. We made something great here. The book is my book, the movie is our movie. Thank you all for coming tonight." He bows, giving Leon a look that says I've spared you for now, but this isn't over yet, then rushes off the stage back into the applauding but confused audience. He pushes his way over to Eliza.

"If you want to be with me, we have to go now."

"What?"

"Your husband called in his goons."

She turns around and sees them.

"Then let's go," she says. He takes her by the hand and they push their way through the crowd.

"Stop them!" shouts the Important Client, pointing a meaty finger. His goons run down the aisles, knocking people into the air.

"This way!" shouts Leroy. José and Eliza follow him through the emergency exit and an alarm goes off. There's a goon waiting in the hall but Leroy downs him with a flying kick and they press on into the lobby, the goons in hot pursuit as they run out of the building and hop inside a beat up station wagon waiting for them at the curb.

"Go, Carlos, go!" shouts Leroy.

"Yes, sir!" he says, speeding off before they get all the doors closed. He makes a left, then a right, then takes them down an alley and makes another right.

"How did you know this was gonna happen?" asks Eliza.

"Because me and José go way back."

"No, I mean how did you know my husband would send his goons after us? How'd you know to have—Carlos is it?"

"Yep."

"How'd you know to have Carlos waiting for us?"

"Eliza," says Leroy, "if there's one thing you should know about me, it's that I'm a student of history. You may not be aware of this, but this ain't exactly your husband's first rodeo. Seven years ago, actor Johan Weissman tried to run off with his third wife, Terra Cotton after they fell in love filming *Rice and Vice*. Nobody's seen either of them ever since, and it ain't 'cause they're living it up in the Bahamas."

"I had no idea," says Eliza. "He never said anything about her."

"It's not public information," says Leroy. "But luckily we've got Carlos on our side. There ain't a computer system on God's green Earth this kid can't hack into."

"I wouldn't say that," says Carlos. "But your husband's servers weren't so tough to crack."

"Why didn't you tell me about all this?" asks José.

"Would it have made a difference?" asks Leroy.

José huffs and stares out the window.

Against her will, Eliza begins to feel like she's being kidnapped and the goons outside are trying to save her. "No," she says. "It wouldn't have."

Carlos pulls onto the highway. It looks like smooth sailing until he notices three black cars with tinted windows weaving through traffic in the rearview. He keeps his cool and slides over to the fast lane, but the black cars are just as dexterous and mirror his every move.

"I think they're onto us," he says.

One car zooms past and cuts in front of them, one starts tailgating them, and another pulls up alongside them.

"We've gotta get out of here," says Leroy.

"I'm trying."

The car beside them rolls down its rear window and a goon in the backseat opens fire, punching holes in the trunk as Carlos zooms ahead and smashes into the car in front of them. They skid sideways and spin the other car into the guardrail, then Carlos swerves into the next lanes and puts some traffic between them. Leroy pulls out his revolver.

"No, Leroy, not in my car—"

"It's okay, Carlos, it's registered. Roll down the windows."

"That's not what I meant! I'm taking the exit, they won't make it." He circles down the off ramp and checks the rearview. The cars are right behind them. At the red light Carlos swerves into traffic disrupting everything, brakes screech and cars smash into poles, everyone's beeping at him, then gunfire and the pickup truck behind them explodes and the goons' cars flip over it. Carlos speeds past a Carlos Jr.'s and turns onto a long, empty valley road. Everybody keeps their eyes out the rear window, but the goons never show up. Looks like the coast is clear.

Leroy pulls out a map and starts giving directions.

In the back, José's still glued to his window. Eliza reaches over and holds his hand. He grips back gently. I'm sorry. I didn't know it would be this way. I won't let you down.

A helicopter buzzes overhead. There's no one else on the road, and they drive on for a while before they realize it's getting louder. Carlos kills the headlights and a searchlight beams down behind them.

"Shit!"

Behind them, the chopper's getting lower and the searchlight's getting closer. Its belly opens up and a giant magnet hangs down over the road. Carlos swerves as the magnet swings by, lifting half the car up but not enough to flip it. The car hurtles down a ditch, smashes through a fence and rumbles into a field. Carlos burns out in the dirt, then drives off in the other direction.

"That's the wrong way!" says Leroy.

"I know."

The helicopter turns around and comes back for them.

"Shit!"

He floors it and pulls his laptop out of the glovebox.

"Leroy, take the wheel!"

Leroy reaches over and steers while Carlos types furiously.

"José, the center console!"

José opens up the center console and unfolds a portable antenna dish. Carlos plugs it into his laptop and José instinctively holds it out the window and points it towards the chopper.

"The magnet's interfering, I need a signal boost!"

Leroy pulls out another cable and plugs it into the cigarette lighter, then José attaches it to an open slot in the back of the dish.

"Alright, let's see how this goes!" Carlos presses enter and the light on the dish turns green. The chopper's getting closer, the magnet starts lifting the back of the car.

"Faster, Carlos!"

"My foot's on the floor!"

Just as they're about to lift off the road, the car slams back down and the whir of the helicopter stops.

"What happened?"

The helicopter crashes to the ground and explodes.

"We did it!"

Carlos and Leroy hi-five, then everyone else hi-fives each other, whooping and hollering as they escape into the night.

Hours later, just before dawn, they arrive at the edge of a great dam straddling a deep canyon. Carlos parks and they get out. José looks up at the Milky Way and wonders what it all means.

"What are we doing here?" asks Eliza.

Leroy lights a cigarette. "Waiting."

José's tempted to ask him for one, but the movie's over. Once again, it's time to quit.

"Waiting for what?" she asks.

"Our point of contact," says Carlos, calling someone on his cell phone.

Leroy exhales and gazes across the canyon at the pink and yellow creeping over the horizon. "After this, you're on your own."

"James? This is Carlos. Yeah, we're—"

Suddenly a horde of SUVs scream over the hills.

"Shit, they found us! Have it ready!" Carlos hangs up and they get back in the car. He speeds out onto the top of the dam, but halfway across he spots another pack of SUVs heading them off on the other side. He slams on the brakes.

"Leroy, get your gun ready!"

"That ain't gonna be enough here!"

The SUVs park in strategic formation and the goons get out and crouch behind them. One goon pulls out a megaphone.

"The jig is up, José! Release Eliza and surrender peacefully! We'll go easy on you, we promise!"

José looks to Eliza for answers.

"Don't listen to them! My husband's word is mud. I'm coming with you, José, no matter what it takes!"

José tears up. If only their love had more time to blossom!

"Psst!"

They look around.

"Down here!" Right at their feet a square of concrete has been jarred loose from the road, held up by none other than James Calahan.

"Hurry!"

José can't believe it, but there's no time for questions. He follows Eliza down the ladder into the dam.

"What about my car?" asks Carlos as Leroy climbs down.

"I'll expense it. Come on!"

Carlos follows him in and shuts the lid.

Down in the belly of the dam, James leads them through a labyrinth of concrete halls lit by caged yellow bulbs. For a while, the only conversation is between the echoes of their interlocking footsteps.

"I didn't build this, you know," says James. Nobody thought he had. "This is my first gig since coming out here. The pay's alright and I know the ghost of my dad told me I gotta head west to build dams or whatever, but I don't know. I've been watching a lot of movies lately and I think I might try my luck at acting. I've always had a dramatic side and—"

"No, don't do it!" says José. "That city is full of evil, it'll—"

"José!" shouts Leroy. "Don't you dare tell this man not to chase his dreams!"

"Well, he did make a movie," says Carlos. "Wouldn't he know?"

"Oh I know alright," says José. "I've seen those bloodsuckers for the vampires they are. They don't value human life like we do, all they care about is—"

"There's more than one road through Hollywood," says Eliza. "Sounds like you took a bad one."

"There's so much I haven't told you about."

"And that's all well and good," says Leroy. "I mean horrible. But if this man's heart is telling him he needs to be an actor then you gotta let him follow it!"

James shrugs. "It was just an idea."

They reach a grotto at the bottom of the dam. A motorboat floats in the cool black water.

"This is where we part ways," says James.

"Where are we supposed to take this?" asks Eliza.

"Downstream," says Leroy. "Follow it to Succotash Bend and you'll be just a couple miles outside town."

"Which town?" asks José.

"You know which one."

Now it's sinking in. "You're not coming?"

Leroy shakes his head. "Me and Carlos have a business to run."

"But what about my husband?" asks Eliza. "He knows you're involved—he'll destroy you!"

Carlos feels chills run through his body. He knew he was getting into hot water, but he didn't think Saguaro Sombrero Solutions Unlimited would be at stake.

"Don't you worry about that," says Leroy. "That's my cross to bear. Like I said, me and Carlos have a business to run."

"But what's our plan?" asks Carlos.

"We can talk about it later, but let's just say our Important Client isn't the only heavy hitter in town."

"Man, you guys are crazy," says James, his eyes full of admiration.

Shouting and footsteps echo down the hallway.

"Go on, get out of here!" says Leroy.

"But what about you guys?" asks José.

James smirks. "Don't worry, I know this place like the back of my hand. We'll just stay two steps ahead of them til they get tired and leave. These bozos are gonna be running in circles all night!"

Leroy scrunches his eyebrows. He thought James would have a better plan than that. José and Eliza board the boat and rev up the motor. James pulls a lever and the steel doors part and let in the dawn's early light. The imperiled lovers putter off downstream, the canyon looming overhead, birds of the desert singing their morning songs. They look back at their friends one last time before the doors close.

15

After a long day's journey, José and Eliza reach Succotash Bend and tie their boat to a broken down, splintery old dock. A trail lined with frayed ropes leads up the canyon wall and they make the ascent. Halfway up, they can barely go on. James didn't leave them any water and they're parched. José collapses onto a flat rock.

"Come on, José, we're almost at the top."

"Si, si, I need rest, Eliza. I'll only be a moment..." He closes his eyes. His head's swimming with voices and images, yet they're all so thin he could blow them away with a whisper. He feels like he's dying in the blistering sun, and maybe he is. Where's a nice puffy cloud when you need it? He feels betrayed. The clouds aren't his friends, they have no loyalty, they don't care if he lives or dies. If only there were a cloud just to look at, just to salivate at, just to hope about, no matter how small or far from the sun, his old friends—just show your faces! Any one of you! Amigos!

He realizes he's moving and opens his eyes. The trail is sliding away from him. He tilts his head back. An old man is pulling him along in a wheelbarrow.

Water splashes his face and he opens his eyes again. His vision's blurred. Someone's handing him something. He takes the bottle and drinks, then rubs his eyes. He's indoors. Eliza and the old man are standing over him.

"There he is. Don't worry, we'll get you back up and running in no time."

"You... I know you..."

The old man scrunches his face and thinks about it. "You do? Do I know you?"

"You gave my friend and I the keys to your gift shop. It's Frank Rodenbelt, right?"

Frank smacks his forehead. "Well ain't this something! How the hell have you been?"

José fills him in on his life's story since they parted ways, starting with his and Leroy's ascent to wealth, then, aided by Eliza, detailing his disillusionment with corporate life, his unexpected success in the poetry scene, his movie deal, their illicit love affair, her husband's wrath, their escape, then when James Calahan enters the picture he circles back to the gift shop, the first days, their tangle with James as a so-called ghost and his father's own ghostly intervention.

"You aren't yanking my chain, are you?"

"No, sir. Mr. Calahan really did return that night. I guess that visit's helped me twice now."

"He was a good man." Frank wipes a tear from his eye. Then it all clicks into place. "Wait a minute. So you're telling me I was being haunted by a phony? That I abandoned my business and my community and turned my life over to Cheesus Grist for nothing?"

Eliza glances at the gory crucifix on the wall. "Well I'm sure it wasn't for nothing..."

"Are you kidding me?" he asks, holding up a Pible. "Do you know how many crazy rules there are in this thing? Cheesus fucking Grist!" He takes the idol down from the wall and carries it out back. He smashes it to pieces, then comes back inside with a smile on his face, dusting his hands off. "Whew. That felt good. Now I ain't gotta worry about going to hell no more." Though José's still weak, Frank takes his hand and shakes it. "Thank you, amigo. If it weren't for you, I might never have learned the truth."

"Perhaps God has intertwined our fates for a reason."

Frank laughs and laughs and tries to say something but keeps on laughing.

Try as he might, José can't convince Frank to accept the return of his gift shop.

"Sure, I was tricked into letting it go. But I gave that store to you boys in good faith, and you sure made a hell of a lot more out of it than I ever could. No, I've moved on with my life. It's yours, José."

And so the next day José and Eliza bid old Frank farewell and head into town with nothing but a jug of water and Frank's dusty Pible. He ain't got no use for that damn book anymore, but José needs it now more than ever. His mama always told him God tests us in mysterious ways, and if he has faith in His Word, everything will work out fine in the end, so he reckons it's time he got around to reading it.

The shop's just as he left it plus a whole lot of dust. The first order of business is to clean up. José and Eliza get to it, but soon he has to go to the bathroom and takes the Pible with him. He sits down and starts reading, and keeps on reading long after his shit's over. The sun goes down and Eliza knocks on the door.

"José? Are you still in there?"

"Oh, si, si!" He sprawls the book on the ground and quickly wipes his ass and flushes the toilet. He opens the door and Eliza looks down at the book and back at him.

"Seriously? I've been working all day cleaning this place up and you've been hiding in there reading?"

"Sorry, Eliza," says José, scratching the back of his head, his mind still flush with Piblical imagery. "Guess I lost track of time."

She sighs. She shouldn't be surprised he's such a bookworm. He is a poet after all. "It's alright. Come on, why don't you show me around upstairs?"

They take some time off to honeymoon before they get the shop up and running. Eliza's access to her bank account has been revoked, but José's savings are more than enough for the time being. He shows her around town and she learns to appreciate the silent beauty of the desert during their daily hikes. The evenings are filled with music and fine dining, or as fine as they can get in this nowhere town, and they always take time to sit out back and watch the sunset. It's a far cry from her honeymoon with the Important Client, a luxurious extravaganza of exotic locales and expensive hotels and gifts, but it's a honeymoon filled with love and promise instead of emptiness, regret, anxiety, and desperate self-reassurance. Day by day, Eliza feels more like herself again, astounded by the degree to which she'd been performing over the years. Eventually she's ready to get to work, and although José would be happy to spend his days loving his love and reading the Pible, he can tell she's starting to crave more structure. He puts in some orders and when the store's all stocked, they open up shop.

Within a few weeks, they've settled into their new lives as if they'd been living them for years. Business is steady and their sex life is magnificent, though José is becoming increasingly adamant that Eliza formally divorce her ex-husband, a proposal she regards as overly idealistic and downright dangerous. Just because he wants to live his life by the rules of some old book, it doesn't mean she has to.

138

Though he tries to hide it, José is becoming increasingly worried about all he's done wrong in his life, the sin he's living in, the possibility of death striking him before he's fully absolved himself before God. He knew things like killing people or running off with another man's wife wouldn't go over well, but there are so many more rules than he thought there'd be! Every day he feels like he's walking a tightrope and falling off over and over again. Manning the cash register, he digs his fingernails into the wooden counter, anxiously eyeing the Pible resting on the shelf underneath. Eliza's scolded him too many times for reading on the job, and he knows it's not fair to let her do all the work, but he needs to keep reading, he needs to find a way out of his torment, a method of redemption, a righteous path out of his life of sin—he wouldn't last two seconds in hell!

Customers have to repeat themselves and wave their hands in front of his face to get his attention. He gives everyone the wrong amount of change, charges the wrong prices, speaks in Spanish instead of American, drips with sweat and emits an odor most foul. Eliza notices and tells him he's gotta stop worrying about that damn book, it's just a story. But it's not so simple, or at least he can't let it be so simple. For one reason or another, it's out of his hands.

One morning, after a particularly disastrous day at work, Eliza tells him to take the day off and get his head right. Snug beneath the covers of their bed, he devours the Holy Word, his mind ablaze with religious passion, hardly aware of the waves of fatigue lapping at its shore. A man possessed, José doesn't notice the sun setting, the food Eliza brings him, the love they make, the Holy Word still glowing before his eyes long after she makes him put the book down. As he lies awake, his lover snoring beside him, ancient scripts write themselves on the ceiling, fading in and out of existence like the roots of trees growing past each other over thousands of years. The scripts swirl around a great pillar descending from a golden sky, the Tower of Bablio at long last returning from oblivion, and as God's false barriers separating the scattered languages of the world dissolve, His Holy meaning shines through.

Eliza wakes to find her lover frothing at the mouth, his tongue lashing out in service of syllables belonging to no language, his eyes turned inward. She tries to make him drink water, then calls the doctor, an old woman named Sara, trained in both Western medicine and ancient indigenous practices. Sara injects him with a tranquilizer to calm him down, then rubs an herb on his head and softly chants, asking the ancient spirits to aid José's recovery. After an hour, he's still unconscious, but she's satisfied with his condition for now. She removes the Pible from his clutches.

"Your husband is a special man. Not just anyone can get sick the way he is. I take it he's been reading this quite a bit lately," she says, idly flipping through the dog eared pages.

"Yes, he's been obsessed. He's owned this store for years but he can barely do anything he's so distracted. I know he thinks it'd be unfair for me to run things by myself, but he's gotten so bad at everything that I made him take the day off to get it out of his system."

Sara chuckles, but there's no smile on her face. "The Pible's not something you can just get out of your system."

"Sure it is. I used to be Gristian."

"Then you know what I mean."

Eliza's confused and wants to argue, but something in Sara's tone makes her pause. Maybe atheism isn't as simple as she thought.

140

For three days and nights José lies in bed, spasmodic and ravaged by sacred dreams. Twice a day Sara visits and does what she can, but tells Eliza that in the end José will only return when he's ready and willing. Whatever spiritual journey he's on must run its course.

When she isn't tending to José, Eliza tries to keep herself distracted tending the store. But as the sun sets each evening, her distress floods back in like the rising tide. Slumped over a bottle of wine, she spends her evenings questioning her every decision, wondering how she got here. Why hadn't her husband's wealth been enough? Why had she let it pave over his horrible personality in the first place? What happened to the carefree, independent girl she used to be? Why the hell did she let this crazy poet drag her out to the desert? She's been around so many artists in her life, she should have known better. Oh, but she loves him, how could she even think that? The questions go on and on and she drinks and drinks, desperately trying to lose herself in the wine's warm embrace, the ripples in her glass, the silence of the desert. But it never lasts. Ensnared by a thousand hooks, she's endlessly dragged away from the world, each clawing thought pulling her deeper into her suffering.

Finally, in the dead of night, José's eyes roll back into place and he returns from his journey. The moon shines in through the blinds casting pale beams across the ceiling like spokes without a wheel. He's starving. He gets out of bed and finds Eliza asleep at the dinner table between an empty bottle and a half-finished glass. He quietly opens the fridge and takes out some chicken, an avocado, a tomato, an onion, a tortilla, and some mole sauce and gets cooking. Eliza wakes up to the sound of sizzling olive oil. José's chopping up the veggies, grooving to a song only he can hear. Without a word, she sneaks up behind him and wraps her arms around his waist.

"You're back."

"Si." He turns around in her arms and holds her in his and they kiss. When they part, he smiles, his eyes full of a warmth she hasn't seen since they first met. "God has forgiven me." He turns back to the pan and dumps the chicken onto the tortilla, then starts piling on the fixings and tops it all off with the mole sauce. He sits down at the table and Eliza throws the bottle out and dumps the rest of her glass in the sink. She pours them both water and joins him.

"You were out for three days."

He chews his food and digests.

"You really scared me, José. I was worried you might never come back."

"I'm sorry, Eliza. It wasn't my choice. God and I had some things we needed to work out."

"José, I'm glad you're trying to make something positive out of what happened, but that was a psychotic episode. You were completely gone, foaming at the mouth, everything!"

José smiles. "I understand your concern. But perhaps we're both right. You see that painting?" He points to the painting on the wall of a desert landscape at sunset.

"Sure."

"What is it?"

"A desert landscape at sunset."

"Si. And yet it is also just paint on a canvas, chemicals reflecting light. There is no desert. It is an illusion."

"So your... talk with God, let's call it. You admit that was just an illusion."

"It was both an illusion and real."

142

Eliza sips her water and decides not to push it any further. She's glad he's back, but what has she gotten herself into?

The next day, Sara visits and confers with José about his experiences, absorbing his interpretations without doubt or approval. At the end of her interview, she asks him if she might speak with Eliza alone, and he takes a blissful walk around town, soaking up every inch of it with fresh eyes.

"So what's wrong with him?" asks Eliza.

Sara laughs. "Wrong and right are inappropriate words for his condition. He has, as we say, sensibilidad sagrada. Sacred sensitivity."

Eliza frowns. "Well he's always been a very sensitive person. Very in touch with his emotions. He is a famous poet after all. But do you really believe him about all this God stuff?"

She shakes her head. "I have my own views about that, but I won't deny him his interpretation."

"Well what are your views then?"

"Why do you need them?"

"Because you're a doctor! I want to know what's really going on."

"Who's to say you don't already?"

"Me."

"Well..." Sara gives in and divulges her thoughts on the matter, how José's condition fits into her own beliefs and conceptions of the great mystery of existence. By the end, Eliza's head is full of even more questions, and in a way, she understands why Sara didn't want to get into it. This is something she'll have to figure out on her own. Before Sara leaves, she gives Eliza a piece of advice.

"From what you've told me, it doesn't seem like either of you saw this coming. But if you think back, I'm sure you'll find this is the path José has always been on. Don't try to pull him off it. You'll only cause yourself more grief."

"Thanks for the tip."

Sara closes the door behind her.

Eliza's furious. Her whole life, she's lived in a world governed by rationality and facts. Now she's the odd one out for not indulging her lover's psychosis.

Over dinner, he tells it to her straight. "I can't keep working at the gift shop with you."

She chews her food and sips her wine, waiting.

"God has called me into His service. I must share what I have learned with the world and spread His Holy Word."

"And what exactly have you learned?"

José smiles. "Oh Eliza, it's not so simple. In my visions there were so many—"

"Then how are you going to share what you've learned with the world if you can't even sum it up over dinner?"

"You don't understand."

"Then help me understand."

But try as he might, the conversation goes in circles. The closest she gets to an answer is that people will pick up the vibe of God's message as José preaches, or maybe the longer he preaches in God's service, the better he'll get at communicating the understandings he received in his visions. As far as she can tell, he has no plan besides joining the local church, leaving her to pay the bills so they don't burn through his savings. In bed, their sex is ferocious and all-consuming. José thinks he's transmitting some of God's love through himself, sharing his understanding through each movement and caress, and Eliza gives it her all to remind him that she's what matters

144

most in his life, not whatever crazy ideas are floating around in his head. But it's no use.

In the morning, he wakes up early and heads on down to church. It's Sunday and the pastor's opening up shop.

"Good morning, Father!"

The pastor unlocks the great wooden doors and turns around. "Good morning, my son. To what pleasure do I owe your early arrival?"

"I have come to devote my life to the Lord."

"Well now! Please, come in." He opens the doors and José follows him in. The church is spacious but simple. The windows are just regular glass, and the only icon is a life-sized crucifix hanging up behind the altar. They walk down the aisle, genuflecting along the way, then reach the front pew and sit down beside each other.

"Let us pray," says the pastor. They kneel, close their eyes, and clasp their hands in prayer. After about a minute, the pastor opens an eye and sneaks a glance at José. His back's straight, his hands are symmetrical, and his lips are moving but hardly make a sound. He can feel José's spirit calling out to the Lord. The pastor has no doubt—this guy's the real deal. After a few more minutes, they stand and genuflect once more, then the pastor puts his hands on José's shoulders and looks into his eyes.

"Your faith is strong, my son. How is it you wish to serve the Lord?"

José tells him about his visions, the scripts on the ceiling, the tower of Bablio reconstructing, what felt like years of pilgrimage in just a few days. The pastor is torn. José is obviously sincere and the pastor wants to trust him, yet his heart is riddled with doubts. Is God trying to tell him something or is the pastor—no, he can't bear to think it. Jealous? No, it can't be that, and yet as soon as the pastor becomes sure his misgivings aren't envy, a voice whispers in his ear. You're in denial. You're afraid this man will take your church from you. No! Then what is it? I don't—God, what are you trying to tell me?

But God doesn't answer and in the end the pastor agrees to take José on as an apprentice. As a test, José is charged with delivering this morning's sermon. He picks out a righteous passage and waits for the crowd to roll in. Since he's not a pastor yet, he doesn't have anything holy to wear. He hopes that won't matter, but he can't help but feel self conscious as the flock starts trickling in. It's like he's back at his first open mic, back before he defeated Pete and became famous. He's surprised. He's done enough readings and speeches that he shouldn't be so wound up, but this is different. This time, God's on the line.

At first José completely bombs. His speech is full of ums and ahs and he stumbles over all his lines. The people yawn and check their watches and glance over at the pastor, looking for an explanation. But then, just as he feels he's lost them, José's scattered mind gives way to serene silence, and without thinking, he says the words he needs to say, reads the words he needs to read, and reveals beneath it all, like gold at the bottom of the clearest lake, the love that selected his every word, his every action, the final echo of God's permission to live. At least, that's how the flock might think of it if they could articulate their feelings. The shift inside them from bored to entranced is so swift and radical, they feel as though they're living through a miracle. They understand now why this man has come to speak to them.

At the end of the service, the pastor thanks José for his contributions and blesses the congregation. All rise and sing one more hymn, then it's time to hang out on the front steps and gossip. José joins them out there to get to know everybody, and not a single one of them fails to shake his hand.

"That was some sermon!"

"I really felt God's presence today."

"Next time I'll make damn sure my kids come with me. You keep on giving sermons like that and there's no way in hell they'll still think church is boring!"

José thanks them all with humility and respect. Some remember him from his time running the gift shop, and he tries his best to dredge up their names, but really he's meeting everyone for the first time.

Standing in the doorway, the pastor smiles in the sunshine. He's glad God sent this man. José's gonna be good for this town.

When José gets back to the shop, Eliza's still asleep. He brews a pot of coffee, chefs up some bacon and eggs, and serves her breakfast in bed.

"Good morning, honey."

"Aw, José!" She gives him a kiss and he lays the tray on her lap and she starts eating.

"I've got good news."

She vocalizes a question mark through her food.

"I'm joining the church!"

She swallows. After all that's happened she's not exactly surprised, but she didn't think he'd do it so quickly. "Oh! That's—that's great!"

"Si, si, but… I'm sorry to leave you to run the store by yourself."

"Oh I'll be fine. It's not like this is the tourist season. You go have fun with your book club!"

"Book club?" For the first time in their relationship, José feels mocked. Eliza shrugs, feigning ignorance.

"That's what people go to church for, isn't it? To hang out with other people who like the Pible, get some analysis from a local scholar, right?"

"People go to church because of their faith! To combine their spirits in reverence of the Lord!"

"Yeah, their faith in the Pible and the Lord who's like the main character."

"You're being ridiculous, Eliza!"

"Maybe I just can't see the picture in the paint."

"What's that supposed to mean?"

"Don't you remember what you said earlier about your visions?"

"That was completely different! Are you—no, I don't want to hear it."

"Hear what?"

"Don't push me, Eliza."

"Oh come on, José."

He takes a deep breath. "Do you... not believe in God?"

"Nope."

"Gah!" He clutches his head. "How could I have not seen this coming? How could I have fallen for someone who denies the existence of the Lord?"

"José, it doesn't have to be a big deal."

"But how can I be a pastor if the woman I love is a heathen?"

"Hey, I used to be Gristian too, you know. Maybe God's testing you. Cheesus says to love everybody, right? Maybe you're not supposed to get off easy falling in love with someone who believes the exact same stuff as you."

Goddamnit. She has a point, but how can he accept her argument, her invocation of the Lord's will in good faith if she doesn't even believe in Him?

148

"Fine. Maybe you're right. I still have much to learn about the ways of the Lord." He slinks out of their bedroom and Eliza finishes her breakfast, puts the tray on the floor, and gets back to her book, *We Got Carried Away* by Olivia Grummond, a tale of two friends who make it big and get carried away.

16

José takes to the pulpit like a fish to water. His time roaming the desert, his financial success, his poetic stardom, his dealings with the devil in the city of angels—it's all been one long march towards his true calling. Church attendance is up three hundred percent and the town is filled with jubilee, its inhabitants reinvigorated by José's message of hope, introspection, and community, but especially by his prophecies. Though vague and abstract, they carry promise of imminent glories, epic battles of the spirit, and incoming salvation for all who believe. Everyone has their own interpretation, and every Saturday night drunken fights break out in the bars over who's right and who's wrong. But the dust always settles and the sun always rises, and Sunday morning, in the presence of José, the brawling disciples realize once again that their interpretations were all incomplete and in fact don't contradict each other in the slightest. God's Word is beyond human language, José tells them, but they've all got to try their best to understand it. His sermons are mere signposts pointing the way, guiding the flock home when they wander astray, returning them to the path of righteousness having learned from their past mistakes, ready to make new ones, trusting in José and the old pastor, but mostly José, and God, to deliver them from ignorance and sin.

One Sunday morning as José's getting ready for church, Eliza reads something disturbing in the paper. "Saguaro Sombrero Solutions Unlimited succumbs to hostile takeover after forty eight-day siege. Michael Sweeney named new CEO."

"Michael Sweeney?! But he's just a suck up! There's no way he could have pulled that off!"

"Not on his own," says Eliza.

The instant José and the Important Client locked eyes at the premiere rushes back in painful slow motion. "I've got to do something."

"No, José. Leroy wouldn't want that."

He balls his fists for the first time since they climbed out of the canyon. "You're right. There's nothing I can do right now." He unclenches his fists. "God, I can't even call him! His phone's probably bugged!"

Eliza feels the urge to hug him but lets it pass.

Years go by. José stays true to his calling. Out in the desert, just outside of town, a great pyramid now stands. He's touched many lives preaching the Word of God, but no matter how much love he gets from his disciples, from Eliza, from God, his heart will never be at ease until—

In the beginning, the pyramid was just going to be an extension of the church. But Roger Ferry, the CEO over at the local quarry, had stopped drinking and turned his life around because of El Profeto's teachings, and believed his savior deserved something more grand. And so he put his crews to work on a stone complex, part castle, part temple, part community college administrator's building. But then El Profeto was stricken with another bout of visions. After five days and nights of prayer and anxious turmoil among his disciples, the new messiah still had not recovered. Roger was becoming completely untethered. Unable to sleep, unable to achieve peace through prayer, binge eating, exercise, hard swork, sex, displays of love and affection to his wife, children, workers, fellow church members, God, even to El Profeto, Roger bought an eighth of marijuana from a dishwasher at the Mexican restaurant and drove out into the desert in the middle of the night to sit on a rock and smoke it all. Sure, it wasn't sobriety, but it wasn't liquor!

He pulled up to his favorite pile of crumbling boulders and rolled a joint on the dashboard, then got out and started towards the boulders. The moon rose over the top of the pile, crowning it, and he stopped in his tracks as he understood that God Himself had just shown him what he must do. He lit his joint, walked back to his car, and wrote down his initial plans for the pyramid on the back of his registration. When he ran out of paper, he started the engine and drove back into town. He spent the whole night and the next day drawing up the blueprints for the new temple, and by evening El Profeto had emerged from his Holy reverie. Upon hearing the news, he rushed over to his bedside and told him of his plans. El Profeto's eyes grew wide, and he smiled a smile full of grace and wisdom, and though weak, reached up to embrace Roger and thanked him for his faith and determination. Towards the end of his visions, El Profeto had found himself at the bottom of a vast pit. Four walls surrounded him, too steep to climb. He was starting to believe he'd die down there until suddenly, after what felt like weeks, a great light enveloped the pit and filled it to the brim, and he floated up high above the ground and the light grew brighter and brighter until at last he awoke.

"Your idea, Roger—it saved me!"

"It did?"

"Don't you understand? The pit I was in was an inverted pyramid! When God gave you the idea for the new temple, it was a test of your faith and my ability to translate His Word. If either of us had failed, well, that doesn't matter now. Once you grabbed hold of that idea and accepted it into your life, the pieces were in place to complete my vision!"

Eliza rolled her eyes but Roger was in awe, and soon construction began, consecrated by El Profeto and bankrolled by the community.

El Profeto now finds himself in the pyramid's inner sanctum, its most central room, deep in prayer. He is seated upon a three-tiered platform draped with a Persian rug, eyes closed, hands clasped, his thoughts and his heart turned towards God. The room is all white—tiles, floor, walls, and ceiling, and there's a short palm tree in every corner. A square moat surrounds the central platform, narrowly separating it from the three entrances at the edges of the room. Besides the sound of rushing water, the sanctum is filled with the ambient drone of the air conditioning system and soft nature sounds from every biome of God's Great Earth piped in through a carefully concealed speaker system. There's a knock on the wall of the entrance directly before him and he opens his eyes. A well dressed young woman is waiting.

"Come in," he says.

She gives a nervous bow and steps across the moat. He stands up and descends from his platform, takes her hand and kisses it, and they sit down beside each other on the bottom tier.

"Genevieve Harrington of the *Desert Sun Digest*, I presume."

"You presume correctly."

"I've been expecting you. In fact, I was praying for you just now."

She blushes. "Sorry I'm late. It's a bit hard finding your way around in here."

"That is by design, in accordance with the manner in which God has given us life."

"You mean it's hard to find your way around in life?"

"Precisely."

"Interesting." She pulls out a tape recorder from her coat pocket. "Do you mind if I start recording?"

El Profeto laughs. "God sees all. Please, as you wish."

She hits record and flips open her notebook, making a note on the philosophy behind the pyramid's confusing design before she begins. This is the biggest interview she's ever done. Her list of questions has gone through dozens of revisions, but after she asks a couple, El Profeto says Why don't we just talk? And so they talk. He's led an incredible life, and his words are full of wisdom, kindness, and a firm, loving opposition to humanity's darkest impulses. She feels like she's discovering just as much about herself as about him. The next time she checks her recorder, two hours have passed.

"I hope I haven't taken up too much of your time," she says.

"On the contrary, I was worried I'd taken up too much of yours!"

They laugh together, then listen to the wonderful sounds echoing throughout the sanctum. He takes her hands in his and switches off her recorder.

"You know, today was the first time I've been interviewed since... my past life. And you're certainly not the first to request one."

"Then why me?"

He smiles and looks deep into her eyes. "The night before you called my secretary, I had a dream. I was walking on a sheet of ice, and below my feet, all of my disciples were frozen in place. I called out to God, let them go! Why must they stay frozen, away from the world? Why

154

must I walk alone? And God's laughter rained down from the sky, and I looked down at the ice and realized it was me, that I was the one keeping them from the world. When I awoke, I resolved to overcome my past and my fears, to no longer settle for guiding my flock in solitude from the rest of Creation, but to do whatever it takes to spread God's Holy Word across the entire world. And so when you called, I knew God was bringing us together."

Genevieve doesn't know what to say. She's never been a part of a prophet's Holy Vision before. Her whole life, she's known God is out there, keeping His loving eyes on the world, but she's never felt His presence in her life so directly.

"Come," says El Profeto. "I'd like to show you something." Holding hands, they cross the room to the back, the only wall without an entrance. He presses his hand to a specific tile, and a green light passes under it. A secret door opens, and they go inside. He presses a button on the wall and it closes behind them. Lit by several tall lava lamps, the secret room is much dimmer than the inner sanctum and filled with the smell of incense. A shaggy rug is sprawled out across the floor and a record player and speakers are set up on a cabinet in the corner. Paintings of naked people from various Piblical scenes adorn the purple walls, and a water bed ripples in its frame.

"What is this?" she asks, her head full of accurate guesses.

"My *inner* inner sanctuary." He lets go of her hand and walks over to the record player. "I come here sometimes when I just need a break from it all. Please, sit down."

She takes her coat off and wraps her tape recorder in it, then sinks into the water bed while he puts on a sensual

R&B album. He grooves to the music for a moment, feeling God's inspiration in every note, then sinks down beside her.

"This is nice," she says.

"I know."

Cautiously, she wraps her arms around him and he returns the favor. They lie there, gazing into each other's eyes until their lips touch and they fall into it, grinding up against each other through their clothes, the water bed sloshing around them like the ocean in a storm.

El Profeto doesn't return to his chambers at the top of the pyramid until midnight, but Eliza's waiting up for him.

"Where have you been?"

"I had an interview today, so my routine took longer than expected."

"An interview?"

"Yeah, an interview."

She takes a bite of her quesadilla. "A religious interview?"

"Sort of."

"You spoke with a journalist."

He can't meet her eye and scuffs the floor with his sandal.

"What the fuck, José? We agreed on this. As soon as that article's published he'll be able to find us."

He clears his throat. "God told me it was time."

"God told you. Really?"

"What do you mean really? Look at where we're living!"

"This place is exactly what I'm talking about! When was the last time you read the Pible?"

"So now you want me to read the Pible! Remember when I first got into it? You were so freaked out—"

156

"Of course I was scared! You were acting like a Pible-fiend and then passed out in bed for three days. The hell is your problem?"

José gazes out the window at the moonlit desert. "I'm just following God's plan."

"That's not good enough."

He shrugs.

"You can't keep avoiding responsibility for your decisions just because you believe in God."

He sighs. "What does that even mean?"

"Stop deflecting."

"Deflecting from what? Who knows why anyone does anything? The only time I really know is when I hear it from God. The rest of the time I'm listening for Him like a hyena on the prairie, like a frog in the night, just sucking it all in, waiting for answers."

"Well what about me, José? Why don't I get any answers?"

"Ask God." He goes into the kitchen, opens the pantry, and digs into a box of animal crackers.

"You know your acid reflux will get better if you stop having midnight snacks."

"But I like them."

"Oh, well in that case I guess God just wants you to keep whining to me about your heartburn."

He eats another animal cracker, then storms off to the bathroom with the box and slams the door.

A few days later, Eliza reads the article in the *Desert Sun Digest*: "A Spiritual Oasis in the American Desert, El Profeto and the New Conquistadors of Peace." The tone of the piece is so fawning, so uncritical, so detached from reality that when she sees Genevieve's picture, Eliza knows right away what happened during their "interview." Yes, she knows all about José's secret room with the waterbed and what goes on in there. They've been cheating on each other with various people for over a year now, but neither of them are in a position to admit it. If it came out, José's religious credibility would be thrown into jeopardy, and if Eliza had to leave the pyramid, where would she go? She's still married to the Important Client, and he'd do his best to ruin any other attempt at starting a new life. Oh sure, maybe she could change her name and move to another country, so in the end she has less to lose than José, but for the time being, life in the desert has still been tolerable, just comfortable enough to outweigh her frustration with the deceit and hypocrisy that surround her.

When she finishes reading, she throws the paper in the trash. What a joke. José's put this entire operation at risk just to stroke his dick and his ego. She tries to go about the rest of her day as usual, reading a book, watching her shows, picking which stocks to buy and sell, which currencies to trade, but her anger morphs into a maelstrom of anxiety ripping away at her no matter how hard she tries to distract herself. Enough is enough. The time has come. She goes into their bedroom and empties the safe into a duffel bag, then piles her favorite clothes and her passport on top of the cash and gold. She takes the elevator down to the ground floor and walks through the lobby with confidence and purpose.

"Where are you off to today, Señora Profeto?" asks the secretary.

"Oh, just giving some old clothes to charity."

"That's very selfless of you. Shall I have someone drive you?"

"No, no, this is something I have to do by myself."

The secretary smiles. "I understand. Enjoy your pilgrimage!"

Eliza rolls her eyes as she passes through the automatic caution doors. How far these wackos have come that every trip outside the pyramid is a pilgrimage. She walks a mile to the station and buys a ticket for the next train to Mexico. Twenty minutes later, she's gone.

17

Today is Yeaster. After his sermon, in honor of Cheesus's resurrection on this Holiest of days, El Profeto has invited the flock to enter the inner sanctum one at a time to receive his Yeaster blessings and have their Pibles autographed. After a dozen disciples, his actions and words become automatic, and he retreats deep into his mind. For three days now, he's assured himself that Eliza hasn't left him. Maybe he's just been too busy and they keep missing each other in the apartment, or maybe she's staying somewhere else in the pyramid because she's still mad at him. But now, on this sacred day, he can deny it no more. When Roger Ferry approaches for his blessing, El Profeto pulls him aside and asks if he's seen Eliza anywhere.

"Not me, but my wife says she saw her in town a few days ago."

In town? Eliza's hardly been to town since they moved into the pyramid! He thanks Roger and waves in the next disciple. Suddenly, the whole pyramid shakes.

"What's going on?"

"Must be an earthquake," says Roger.

It shakes again and the disciples scream.

El Profeto picks up the receiver to the pyramid-wide intercom. "Please everyone, remain calm." He presses a button and his nasally Spanish cover of "What's Going On?" by Garvin May comes on to calm the people and remind them that even he doesn't know what's going on sometimes, and that's okay.

The music stops and a new voice crackles through the speakers.

"Attention! Disciples of El Profeto! This is God speaking!"

The uproar ceases in the presence of God.

"You have sinned in the eyes of the Lord! My eyes! You're making them sting, you're sinning so badly. Stop! At once!" The pyramid rumbles again. "You feel that? Y'all have five minutes to leave before I blow this place up, and ain't nobody's coming back like Cheesus!" God hangs up and the music comes back on. Half the flock stampedes and the rest tumble in the crush or stand their ground stunned like boulders in a stream.

Roger Ferry looks to his savior, but El Profeto's just as confused as anyone. He presses the receiver and the intercom screeches for a second. He gulps.

"I don't know whether that was God or not, but I guess we should leave." He drops the receiver and hops down from his platform as the music comes back on.

"You don't know?" a disciple shouts at a television broadcasting the inner sanctum.

"It could be terrorists!"

"It could be the CIA!"

"But what if that really was God?"

"Then El Profeto's a fake and we're being punished!"

The exodus continues, the crowd flooding out into the parking lot, angry and scared.

El Profeto puts his hand to the wall beside one of the potted palms and a secret door opens. He waves Roger over.

"Come on, it'll be faster."

Roger hesitates, then follows him in. They walk down a long set of stairs going straight to the bunker under the parking lot. When they reach it, El Profeto opens the fridge, cracks open a tamarind soda, and sits down in a comfy rocking chair.

"You can have one too if you want."

"Shouldn't we go up?"

"We're good in here, right?"

"I don't know, the bunker might still count in God's eyes."

"If he can see us."

"Of course he can see us."

"I meant if that voice really was God." El Profeto takes a long sip.

Roger checks his watch. "I guess we've got a few more minutes." He opens a mole soda and they drink in silence. It tastes better that way. When they're finished, El Profeto puts both their bottles in the recycling bin, then opens a manhole in the ceiling.

"See you on the other side." He disappears up the ladder.

"El Profeto! That's not the exit!"

But El Profeto doesn't listen. Roger opens the exit and climbs out into the sun.

"Hey everyone, I found Roger!" shouts the secretary. Those nearby cheer, but before word can really spread, everyone's distracted by El Profeto's emergence onto a platform beneath one of the parking lot lights.

"Attention, amigos!"

The crowd simmers down.

"One way or another, it appears God has spoken! Please, return to your homes."

"But what about the pyramid?"

"So that really was God?"

El Profeto laughs. "God or not, if anything should happen to this pyramid, know that buildings may rise and fall, but nothing can shake our faith! Please, take precautions! Go home! And if any be without a home to return to, may they be welcomed in the homes of thy neighbors. And in the worst of cases, should any of thee find thyselves forced to book a hotel room, hangeth on to the receipt, and we shall reimburse thee at the earliest opportunity!"

The reassured crowd cheers, and they all get in their cars and head back into town. El Profeto watches them drive off in a cloud of dust, and in the end only Roger remains.

"Want a ride?" he shouts from the ground.

"Yes, thank you!" El Profeto goes back inside the lightpost and starts climbing down. As he descends there's a horrific groan, and he hangs on for dear life as the lightpost topples over. He's smacked against the inside and everything goes black.

He wakes up in an unfamiliar room. The curtains are drawn but daylight beams in through a gap in the middle. There's a glass of water on his nightstand and he takes a sip. His face hurts, his ribs are killing him. Just sliding the covers off feels like ripping off a hundred bandaids. He peeks under his shirt, his pants. It's all black and purple. He hopes he hasn't broken any bones. He carefully pulls the covers back over himself and goes back to sleep.

Roger and someone else are standing over him. Roger and Dr. Abel. He remembers Dr. Abel from the early days. A true man of God. He hasn't seen him much around the pyramid, but he's glad he's here.

"There he is," says Roger. He gently brings his hand to El Profeto's cheek. "You're in good hands." He nods to Dr. Abel and leaves the room.

"What happened? Is the pyramid still standing?"

"Yes, yes. It appears the lightpost you were climbing down from hadn't been constructed properly and came loose. You have some cracked ribs and heavy bruising, but you're lucky to be alive."

"I suppose God still has a plan for me."

"Yes, well, unfortunately I don't think that plan involves you going back to the pyramid. A bunch of goons showed up later and seized control."

"Goons? When? Who sent them?"

"I don't know who sent them, but they're very professional looking. They got there just a few hours after we left. If that voice of God was just some trick, it wasn't in their favor. I hate to say it, José, but those goons are looking for you. They already stopped by, but Roger sent them on their way. Still, Roger says some folks are aware that he stayed behind to give you a ride. Under ordinary circumstances, I would urge you to remain in bed at least another couple of days, but seeing as this situation might pose further danger to your life, as your doctor my recommendation is that you leave town as quickly and discreetly as you can. Roger has expressed willingness to aid you in that endeavor."

"But what about my home? What about my disciples?"

"José, I don't know who you crossed before you came here to preach, but they've got money and, it seems, the government's blessing to hold you accountable by any means necessary. So don't worry about any of that right now. You're a good man and an inspiring teacher. The congregation will figure out how to get by without you. If you'd like to write a letter explaining your absence, I can read it before them all at the first opportunity."

José thinks it over. Looks like Eliza was right about that article. But if he's not safe in the middle of nowhere, where the hell is he supposed to go?

"Thanks, Dr. Abel. I'll write something."

"Great! I'll leave you be for now." He places a bell on the nightstand. "Give this a ring when you're ready to go."

"Sure thing."

Dr. Abel looks him over one more time, sorry he can't do more to help.

José spends the whole afternoon writing his letter, scrapping draft after draft, scouring the depths of his mind for the right words and the right way to say them. Being a religious leader has meant so much to him, it's almost as hard to express how he feels right now as it's been to translate the Word of God into the human tongues of American and Spanish. But eventually, he gets the job done. He rings the bell and the brass gleams in the amber light of the setting sun. Dr. Abel and Roger Ferry return and he reads them his letter. After all, they too are among his:

Disciples, Amigos, Familia,

My heart is heavy, my body is bruised. Some of my ribs are cracked, but already I can feel God's nimble fingers threading them back together. Yes, maybe you've heard. An accident happened after you left. The lightpost from which I directed you all away from the pyramid was not properly constructed. The base came loose and the whole thing fell over while I was still climbing down. This accident was not Roger Ferry's fault, though I must confess to you all before God that I cursed his name on the way down because yes, he was the architect after all. He did supervise the construction of the pyramid, including its parking lot. Really, such an accident should not have happened. But no, all that matters is it's over, I'm safe, I'm healing. Unfortunately, I cannot be with you at the moment due to the current persecution of our faith by malevolent goons sent by the forces of evil. Please, return to your daily lives and keep your noses clean. The pyramid shall rise again. Let it stand tall in our souls. Don't let these goons take your town from you and trample your faith! Fight! Fight! Fight!

In exile, I too will be fighting. Every day my heart shall long to be with you, burning for the day we can again be scorched by God's love together in peace! But for now, hang tight and get these goons out of here in some kind of secret revolt. You probably don't have to kill them all, I bet you could do something like maybe put a bunch of pies in the windows of the jailhouse, hide in the bushes, and push those motherfuckers in when they come sniffing around. Or go to the Russians, or Panamanian bankers or something, somebody. Or if all else fails, maybe you can move our operation to Vegas and get in on a piece of the action over there, do some major soul saving. I'm just spitballing, but I'm sure Roger can build you all a new pyramid when he gets back, one more glorious than any this continent has ever seen! You'll fit right in.

So go forth, for the Kingdom, the Power, and the Glory are Yours, now and forever, Amen.

Blessings of Love to All,
José Jones
A.K.A.
Yours Truly,
El Profeto

Roger's crying, grateful for the trust José has placed in him to lay the foundations for God's Kingdom wherever he needs to, even in Las Vegas, the city of vice and sin. Whatever happens, he will always remember this moment.

Dr. Abel is mystified and worried by Roger's reaction. José totally set him up as a scapegoat. And to incite the town to fight back against the goons? People are going to get killed! How is that the way of Grist? He shakes his head. Oh well. Best thing to do as a doctor and a Gristian is to get him out of town.

"El Profeto, this letter is truly something. I'll be happy to read it to everyone when the time is right," says the good Doctor.

"As soon as possible."

"As soon as it's safe."

"Maybe just a little sooner if it's possible, though."

Dr. Abel's intelligence feels insulted, his medical expertise overlooked, but he holds his tongue. José heaves himself out of bed and immediately falls, knocking over the lamp on his nightstand. Roger and Dr. Abel rush to his aid.

"No, no, I can walk on my own." But he can't so they toss his arms over their shoulders.

"Are you sure you're ready to leave?" asks Dr. Abel.

"Absolutely. They could search this place any minute. Just throw me in the trunk with a blanket and some water, I'll be fine."

"What about a pillow?" asks Roger.

"Sure, that'd be nice."

Roger hurries off to fetch everything and Dr. Abel walks José down the hall, down the stairs, and into a rocking chair in the coatroom behind the kitchen. They wait while Roger goes out and loads the trunk. When he gives the signal they hobble out back and slot José in with the speed and precision of a pit crew on race day. With just a nod, Roger and Abel part ways. Roger hops in front, the lights come on, the engine starts, and he drives off with the same calm as a morning drive to work. Abel doesn't even watch, he's already back inside.

Roger cruises through the streets, obeying every traffic law. The goons are out in force, sitting outside restaurants eating ribs and pizza and drinking beer, walking around with ice cream cones and balloons and more beer. At least they're helping the economy. Wait, if the pyramid's closed, but these guys are shopping everywhere, which helps the economy more? Roger does the math and realizes the economy is actually a competition between the town and the pyramid. This whole time, he'd been so focused on the pyramid that he forgot about the bigger picture. Everyone did. The pyramid was where the action was happening. Now, forced back into their old way of life, everyone must ask themselves: What is God telling us?

The escape goes off without a hitch. When they're far enough into the desert, Roger pulls over and lets José out of the trunk.

"Come on, why don't you lie down in the back?"

"It's alright, I'll ride shotgun and lean the seat back."

Roger would feel more at ease if he lay down in the back, but El Profeto's the boss. They get back in the car and set off again.

"So where to?" asks Roger.

José thinks about it. "No hotels. No motels. Nothing that would leave a paper trail, no unusual activity."

"You think they're that thorough?"

"I don't know."

They drive in silence.

"My apartment."

"You have an apartment?"

"Yeah, back in LA. I've still been paying rent this whole time. I signed a five year lease like a fucking idiot."

"Well it doesn't seem so stupid now!"

José sighs. "You're right. I'm too hard on myself. Still, we should approach it with caution. My Biggest Enemy knows I haven't been there in years, but he might still have someone watching it."

"Your Biggest Enemy? Is that who sent all those goons?"

"I think so."

Roger shakes his head. "I don't understand. You're a great person!"

"There's a lot you don't know about me."

As they drive through the night towards the city of angels, José tells Roger his life's story, starting from his fateful friendship with Leroy. With the exception of the journalist he fucked the other day, José has been notoriously tight-lipped about his past since becoming El Profeto, telling all who ask that he's too busy right now, even during private dinners and intimate post-coital moments. By the time he gets to his dealings with the Important Client and Leon Primrose, Roger starts to understand why José's been so keen to leave it all behind. Far from containing the scandalous seeds to his downfall, as all curious disciples secretly feared when their questions were brushed aside, José's story deepens Roger's faith in and respect for him, not just as an interpreter of God's Word, but as a fellow human being who's strived and suffered, who's risked and won and lost it all and carried on anyways. For the first time, Roger sees José not just as his savior, but as his friend.

18

They pull up to José's apartment at two in the morning. There's a rare thunderstorm menacing the city. The palm trees are blowing sideways, the waves are crashing down with unusual violence, and all the homeless people are tucked away in their tents as the rain fills the gutters and floods the streets. If anyone's staking this place out, tonight's the perfect night to sneak in. With Roger's coat draped over them both, they hobble over to the front door. José's key still works. They pass the empty front desk and take the elevator up. When they reach the fifth floor, José's confused about his apartment number. Was it 513 or 531? Waking someone up in the middle of the night is the last thing he needs right now. Panicked, he glances back and forth at the two arrows on the wall:

<- 501-515, 516-530 ->.

"Which one is it?" asks Roger, smelling something funky.

"I don't know, I forgot! Oh God I've got them mixed up, I'm sorry Roger—"

"You don't remember your number?"

"It's either 513 or 531 but we can't just go trying people's doors! We're stuck! I'm so sorry—"

"Look, El Profeto, good news! 531 doesn't exist!"

José looks again and calms down. "You're right. Oh, thank God, you're right." They trudge over to 513 and unlock the door. They take their shoes off inside and turn on the lights. The place is exactly as he left it, but covered in three inches of dust. Then the stench hits them, and José notices a pile of paper on the ground. Did something die in

170

there? Yo, take out the trash. Are you alive? Hello? Holy shit, I have asked you five times already! Whatever it is, clean your shit up! José's stomach sinks as he realizes what it is. This place might not be habitable after all.

"What's that smell?" asks Roger, covering his face.

José opens the fridge and the stench nearly blinds him. He slams it shut and braces himself against the counter, coughing like crazy. "Open a window," he wheezes.

Roger opens two right away, neither of them caring about the rain splattering in through the screens.

"Three years, at least."

"Since you were last here?"

José nods. "I should have come back and cleaned up before I got chased out of town."

"It was a stressful time for you. Nobody expects to get run out of town."

"Thanks Roger," he says, though his kind words aren't much comfort. He picks up an official looking envelope from the pile of papers and opens it.

Attention Resident:

We have received numerous complaints of a foul odor emanating from your apartment for over a year now and have already issued three warnings. Since you have not heeded our warnings, we have no choice but to quadruple your rent to cover the cost of the neighbors you keep driving away. We think this is a pretty fair deal, since you're the only one in the building loyal enough to sign a five-year lease. The increased payments will be deducted from your account every month until you have dealt with the odor.

Sincerely,
Management

José wipes a tear from his eye.

"What's wrong?" asks Roger.

"I could have been dead in here and they didn't even check on me. Just used me for my money."

"You didn't call them when they tripled your rent?"

"No, Roger, I was busy. Besides, I'm pretty loaded. Stuff like that's not really on my radar anymore." To make matters worse, José spots his bonsai tree, wilted and frayed by the window. He starts sobbing and runs over and hugs it. "I'm so sorry! Oh God, what have I done?" The dead leaves brush against his face and fall to the ground, and his tears water the arid soil.

"It's alright, El Profeto, we can go buy a new one tomorrow."

But José only sobs harder, and Roger wonders whether he said the wrong thing. With no end in sight to José's sorrow, Roger tries to do something about the fridge. He opens the cabinet under the kitchen sink and gets some surface cleaner and gloves out, plus there's still a roll of paper towels on the counter.

"Don't bother, Roger, that's not gonna be enough."

"Really?" he opens the fridge and quickly closes it, gagging. He leans over the sink but the nausea passes and he drinks some water.

José can't help but laugh at him. "Told you. Come on, I've got a better idea." He goes into his bedroom and rolls a dolly out from under the bed. He skateboards on it into the kitchen and clips himself in the ankle when he gets off.

"Ow!"

"Are you okay?"

"Yeah, let's get this thing out of here."

Roger wiggles the fridge out of the corner and unplugs it.

"Alright, lift it up," says José.

"Wait, where are we taking it?"

"There's a dumpster out back."

"Well let's tape it up first. I don't want the doors swinging open and dumping that shit everywhere."

"Good thinking." José finds some duct tape in his arts and crafts supply cabinet and wraps four layers around the whole fridge. Roger props the front door open, then they heave the fridge up onto the dolly and roll it out into the hall. They go back in and put on their shoes, then roll it over to the elevator and hit the down button. An apartment door opens and a man in an undershirt and boxers glares at them.

"So it's you, huh? Finally showing your face after all these years!"

"I'm sorry, sir, I was away, we're throwing it out right now—"

"I don't give a fuck! You owe me, motherfucker, you owe all of us!" He runs back inside and comes back with a camera and snaps a pic right as the elevator doors open. They push it inside and he snaps a couple more.

"You're not getting away with this!"

The doors close and Roger hits the G button. They pinch their noses and hold their breath until the doors open and they book it out of there. They roll it down the hall and to the left, then José leans backwards into the back door and steps out into the pouring rain. They heave it over the ridged aluminum separating the tile floor from the gritty concrete and roll it up to the dumpster. They open the lid, and on the count of three they pick the fridge up from the bottom and lift. José's barely doing shit but luckily Roger can deadlift six hundred pounds. At last, the fridge topples in with a loud clang. They close the lid and hi-five.

"Yo, what the hell?" A homeless man emerges from a mess of blue tarp, rubbing his head. "That was fucking loud!"

"Sorry, sir, we were just—"

"Hey man, I live here! You really had to do that in the middle of the night?"

"It was an emergency," says Roger.

"Emergency my ass—" He starts sniffing, then recoils. "The hell did you throw in there? You guys serial killers or something? That's nasty, man."

"Sorry, I was gone for a few years and left some things in the fridge."

"What? You mean this whole time, there's been an apartment up there I could have been squatting in?"

"Well, no, that's not allowed—"

"Aw shit!" He kicks the dumpster and hurts his foot, then hops around for a bit til it's better. "God fucking damnit! This smell's too much, man. Can't you guys throw that out somewhere else?"

"Sorry, sir. The deed is done," says Roger.

"Motherfuckers!" The homeless guy grabs his tarps and carries them off in search of a new alley.

The apartment still stinks like a fresh coffin so they douse the place with air freshener and light José's entire collection of scented candles. They blowtorch, then scrub everything around where the fridge used to be, wipe all the counters, mop all the floors, and dust. Roger offers to go buy groceries and José gives him his spare keys. Roger knows he'll just give them back when he returns with the food, but this means something.

The rain's stopped now. José stands by the window and watches Roger cross the street, get back in his car, and drive off. What a good friend he has in Roger. Indeed,

174

where would life have taken him without all the great friends he's met along the way? He wonders how Leroy's doing. And Carlos, and the MC at the open mic, whatever his name was, and Renée and Clyde and the other Fighting Mambos, even though none of them came to visit him in the hospital. His people out in the desert are cool too, but they're more disciples than friends.

José remains without doubt that his visions were from God Himself, but he's glad to be back in LA. That El Profeto schtick was getting old. He's grateful and all, and he's had plenty of good times, some of the best times of his life even, or like, the highest points at a thing in life, like the best sermon he ever gave, or the most people he ever felt deeply connected with in the same room, or the most people he's ever had sex with at once, or the best orgasms he's ever had, or the most orgasms he's ever had in one night, or twenty-four hours because there was one time that was the most of them all but it was like, dusk to dawn. Or the best jam session he's had, even the best inner sanctum. Like, praise God! But by the end, it all felt too easy. Like, what's the point if there's no challenge? He was sleeping longer, sixteen hours a day if he could. In dreams, he swam and flew and spoke with the dead. He ran from friendly assassins and savage detectives, crossed plains of ice, and walked on the moon. He died many times. Sometimes death was waking up to Life as El Profeto, but sometimes he persisted beyond his demise, a floating observer unacknowledged by the living. He'd watch helpless as the years flew on without him, the world changing in ways he longed to be a part of. He stood outside moments that were gut-wrenching, heart-breaking, shocking, and banal. He'd awake with a sense of confusion and spend the rest of the day figuring out what it all meant, giving inquisitive, open-ended sermons and cornering anyone who showed up in the dream to squeeze every last interpretation out of them.

He lights a cigarette. Down the street, there's a billboard showing a shadowy figure looming over a young man writing in his journal in front of a factory, surrounded by giant bags of popcorn. Lightbulbed lettering reads POPCORN LEGACY and fancy cursive reads *a Leon Primrose Production*, the Big Time Studios logo tastefully placed in the bottom right corner. José takes a nice long drag and chews that one over. So Leon's got Pete. He squints. Upon closer inspection, Pete's actually starring as himself. Wow. Already this movie's shaping up to be a pile of crap. Maybe after this Pete'll stop walking around with such a massive chip on his shoulder about that popcorn guy. Nah, José doubts it. If anything, this movie will solidify Pete's insecurity even further, probably for the rest of his life. He takes another drag and prays.

"God, if the Pible's supposed to help me do better at loving all my neighbors, shouldn't Your teachings really be kicking in right now? 'Cause honestly, I'm finding this whole situation hilarious. What's the deal? Love, José. I mean, amen." He takes another drag. There's a bang and he snaps around. Another one. Bang. Bang. Someone's kicking down the door. For a split second he wonders if it's God's teachings, then comes to his senses, stubs his cigarette in the bonsai soil, and hides behind the couch.

"Time's up, Mr. Jones!" The intruder sniffs the air. "Aw, what the hell happened in here? Are you a serial killer?"

José peeks around the corner and gets a glimpse of him. The intruder's a seven foot tall baldy with a bionic eye wearing a trenchcoat. He walks with slow steps, gun drawn. José circles back and crawls around the couch only to bump headfirst into the intruder's leg. He looks up into the barrel of the gun.

"Get up."

José slowly stands up and the gun follows him.

"See that?" He points to a small red light on the trim by the doorless doorway. "Motion detector, put it there three years ago. After what you did to my Client, did you really think you could come back to this city and everything would be alright?"

José looks at the ground, ashamed. "I guess not."

"Then why are you here?"

"What do you care?"

The intruder chuckles. "Just had this case on the backburner all these years. Guess I'm curious what it's really about. I heard you ran off with his wife, and honestly, I'm impressed. Not everyone's got those kind of balls."

"Do you get along well with your Client?"

"Don't even try. Come on." He grabs José by the shoulder and marches him out the door. "But for the record, no. That guy's a douche. Big long job like this and he's barely paying me more than my usual."

"How much is that?"

He tells him as they arrive at the elevator.

"I'll double it."

The detective laughs and pushes the down button. "With what money?"

"I left town rich and I've only gotten richer. Let me write you a check and we can forget all about this."

The elevator doors open.

"Cash."

"Well I don't have very much cash right now, and my debit card has a limit."

The detective shoves him inside and hits G. José waits until the doors close.

"Alright, how about I give you as much cash as I can withdraw and write you a check for the rest." José pulls out his checkbook and a pen, ready to sign.

The detective is silent. The doors open and he marches him through the lobby and out into the street in his bare feet.

"Come on, sir, please! I don't want to die!"

The detective drags him by the collar and lets him go in front of an ATM.

"Oh, thank you, sir, thank you, you won't be disappointed—"

"Triple."

"Huh?"

"Get your max out and write me a check for triple what my Client's paying me."

Ay caramba! José can afford it but that's a lot of money!

"Fine! Fine! I'll do what you want. My life is priceless."

"Then I guess you'd be fine paying quadruple."

"No, sir, I would not. You already made your offer and I accepted. I don't like people who don't keep their word."

"José, you're already paying me to go against my word."

"Exactly."

The detective holds the gun to José's head. "Quadruple."

In the end, José ponies up and goes free. Dejected and elated, he walks back to his apartment, careful to avoid the needles and broken glass. He reaches the entrance right as Roger gets back, his arms full of groceries.

178

"What are you doing out here?" asks Roger. "Where are your shoes?"

"I'll tell you in a minute."

They take the elevator and go back to the apartment.

"What the hell happened?" asks Roger, putting the bags down on the counter. José picks up the smashed door and jostles it back into its frame, but the hinges are torn.

"Turns out someone was keeping an eye on this place after all." That reminds him. He plucks the motion detector from the trim and throws it in the trash. "Motion detector."

"But what happened? Did you kill the guy or what?"

"No, I just paid him off."

Roger raises his eyebrows. "And what's stopping him from taking the money and turning you in anyways?"

José shrugs. "He doesn't seem like the type. Besides, I paid him pretty well."

"How much?"

He tells him.

Roger's jaw drops, then he scratches his head. "But then why didn't you help bankroll the pyramid?"

"Because it wouldn't have been my place. That would have been like chipping in for my own Gristmas gift!"

"No it wouldn't, that pyramid was for everyone!"

Now it's José's turn to raise an eyebrow and Roger has to admit—that lofty ideal is not exactly in line with the true reasons the pyramid was built.

"Look," says José. "I'm not one to invest willy nilly on other people's passion projects. Anyone can amass wealth if they get lucky taking risks, but you need tact and an iron will to hang onto it."

As a fellow businessman, Roger's impressed, but he's still pissed José didn't chip in. Like he literally encouraged him with a Holy Vision and by far got the most use out of it! Roger put his entire life savings on the line building that thing and even convinced the town to go into debt! He wonders what God or Cheesus would say, then sighs when he's forced to acknowledge that José probably talked it over with them already so it's really on him to figure out how this was all part of Their plan.

They unpack the groceries, then make some avocado toast and call it a night. The place is chilly with all the windows open, so José invites Roger to share the bed with him. Roger says it's fine, he can just sleep on the couch, but José insists, then begs him, he's so cold he won't be able to sleep. Roger gives in and climbs under the covers.

"See? Much better, right?"

But despite the meager warmth of José's scrawny body, Roger's frozen with embarrassment and fear. José slides his skinny arm over Roger's side and starts rubbing his belly.

"What are you doing?"

"Shh... Relax..."

But Roger can't relax. Sure, José's hand against his skin is soothing, but inside his head dozens of voices are calling him a fag or pleading with him to stop his sinful ways. This is what he's been working away, drinking away, praying away, this is what he's been running from. And now the man who's helped him most in his life, who set him on God's path, is stroking his penis with the virtuosity of a first chair violinist.

"Stop, this is wrong..." he says without moving a muscle.

"Shh... " José disappears under the covers and starts sucking on it.

"But what about the Pible? Oagh!"

José slides his mouth off Roger's dick with a plop. "It's cool, Roger, God didn't really mean any of that stuff."

"But it's in the Pible!"

"Sure, but it was like a typo or something, like Chinese whispers. Seriously, Roger, I talked to Him when I was asking about my dead brother and He said it was cool and that my bro just barely squeaked into heaven, and all the points against him were just 'cause of some other stuff he did when he was running with a bad crowd. Not 'cause he was gay."

Roger lifts up the covers and looks José in the eye. "You're serious? You're not just making this up so you can do whatever you want, right?"

José rolls his eyes. "Come on, Roger, a bunch of us were already doing this back at the pyramid. If you believed me about all my other visions, why not this one?"

Roger thinks about it and starts nodding, then flips José over and plows him til the sun comes up, tears streaming down his face.

In the living room, a leaf sprouts from a branch of the bonsai tree.

19

Months go by and José and Roger settle into their new life as lovers in Los Angeles. They don't answer the phone and José never leaves the apartment without putting on a beret, sunglasses, and a fake nose and moustache. But for Roger, life feels normal for the first time since puberty. Now that he's not living in hell, shoving down his thoughts and urges by any means necessary, begging God to cure and forgive him—things are pretty chill. They buy all their food at the organic market, take long walks on the beach, visit independent boutiques full of overpriced knick knacks, lift weights at the local gym—Roger has to teach José everything from scratch—and even attend open mics, though they hang out in the back where no one will talk to them. On these excursions José takes extra care with his disguise, stuffing a small pillow down his tucked-in shirt and wrapping a chic scarf around his bony neck. A lot of new poets have come onto the scene since José's day, some of them are even good. But as much as he enjoys the passive anonymity of spectating, José leaves every open mic itching to get back in the game.

"There's just so much I could expand on, so much I've learned, so many ways my style could completely change—"

"Come on, José, do we really have to do this all over again?"

"But I'm getting better at disguising myself! If you didn't see me put this on, could you even tell it's me?"

Roger sighs. "Probably not. But you've got fans, José, dedicated ones. Real nutjobs, in some cases. No matter how hard you try to come off as someone different, once you spend enough time in the limelight they'll be sure to sniff you out. You're a one of a kind, the greatest poet this city's ever seen! At least that's what your fans used to say. Were they wrong?"

José slumps and keeps his eyes on the sidewalk. "No."

Roger feels bad for him. José might have set him free, but now he's the one who has to live a lie. "Come on, I'm hungry." They walk over to a lot where some food trucks are parked. Roger's starving after standing around listening to those poets for three hours. They line up at the Tex-Mex truck. Roger orders smoked ribs, and in a flash of delight, confusion, and embarrassment, José realizes Leroy's the cashier. He looks away as Roger hands over a ten, but Leroy squints at him.

"What's that, a disguise?"

"We were just at a soirée," says Roger, smooth as butter. He has no idea what a soirée is, it just sounded gay enough to fit José's disguise.

"A soirée, huh? Is that like a costume party?"

"Yeah."

"Well what do you really look like?"

"I—I'm shy," says José, hiding behind his scarf.

"Oh come on, José, you really think you're fooling me with that crap? And here's your ribs, partner." He hands the plate over and Roger digs in. José lowers his scarf and meets Leroy's eye. He takes his nose and glasses off.

"Hi, Leroy."

Leroy looks around. "Let's catch up out back, huh?" He switches the sign to Closed and shuts the window.

"I don't think that's a good idea," whispers Roger, his mouth dripping with barbeque sauce.

"Come on, Roger, it's Leroy"

Roger's still not sure but it's José's call. They go around back. Leroy unties his apron and tosses it over the door. He lights a cigarette, then offers one to José. To Roger's shock, he accepts.

"Come on, José, you've been doing so well—"

"I'm smoking today, Roger." He lights it and takes a defiant, titanic puff.

Leroy chuckles. "I always knew you were a little light in the loafers. Good for you, man."

José looks himself over. "You're right, I guess I have lost some weight since we last saw each other."

Leroy and Roger laugh.

"You know, you could have called or something. Figured you'd be a little more grateful for that stunt we pulled."

"I'm sorry, Leroy, this detective broke in the first night we got back and we've been playing it super safe since then. But I'll never forget the night you helped me escape. I owe you my life."

Leroy furrows his brows. "Which night? The one at the dam?"

"Yes."

"Oh, come on, I ain't talking about that!"

"Then what?"

He looks at both of them, but neither of them get it. "Y'all really thought God Himself told you to clear out of that pyramid?"

"That was you?" cries Roger through a mouthful of meat.

"Yes, sir, on the loudspeaker anyhow. Carlos was the one that hacked your system and activated the earthquake counteraction protocols."

"But why?" asks José.

Leroy smacks his forehead. "Come on, really? You had a bunch of bogeys heading your way and nothing short of an act of God was gonna get you out of there in time to miss 'em."

"But how'd you know they were coming?"

"You think you're the only one who's been on the run since that premiere? Me and Carlos lost everything, man, had to lay low and start from scratch. He's the one running this truck, or trucks now. I'm just a cook. And we're still not off the hook, so Carlos keeps tabs on our Old Friend. Has a few worms in his computer system, makes sure we know what he's gonna do before he does it. Saved our asses more times than I can count."

José sighs. "I'm sorry, Leroy. I didn't want you to get wrapped up in this—"

"Hey now, I did what I did because it was the right thing to do." He bends down and stubs his cigarette on the ground. "Well, I gotta get back to work." He puts his apron back on. "Say, you didn't forget your promise, did you?"

José gulps. "I didn't."

Leroy gives him a curt nod and a sad look, then climbs back into the truck.

"What's he talking about?" asks Roger as they walk back to the car.

"Nothing."

"It didn't seem like nothing."

"Just something I've been putting off for a while. It's not important."

Roger still wants an answer but he doesn't push it any further. "Is Leroy your ex or something?"

"No, no," says José, laughing to reassure him, to lighten the mood, to move on from the promise. "I told you, we were business partners."

"I remember. Just..."

"What?"

"Sometimes people leave things out when they tell stories. Come to think of it, I barely know anything about you from before you guys met."

José sighs. "Let's just go home."

José takes a siesta when they get home and Roger tries to relax and watch some TV, but something's nagging at him. He switches it off and paces the room, then slips out and walks over to a phone booth with cracked glass and sticky buttons. He hesitates, but he's desperate to hear some news from back home, to talk to someone familiar, so he slots in some coins and calls Dr. Abel. It rings on and on.

"Hello?"

"Dr. Abel!" His heart is pounding.

"Roger? Where are you?"

"I'm at a phone booth."

"Where?"

"I can't tell you."

"Come on, Roger, those goons left months ago."

"I can't, Dr. Abel, their boss might have the whole town bugged!"

"That's why I bought a new phone."

"But what if it's at the switchboard level?"

Dr. Abel sighs. "Fine. Are you safe?"

"Definitely, man, life's good! I'm gay!"

Dr. Abel laughs his ass off. "Cheesus Grist, Roger, you think I didn't know?"

"You did?"

"I'm a doctor, of course I knew."

"I didn't know doctors could tell that kind of thing."

"I'm kidding, Roger, everyone knew. I bet you're feeling a lot better now."

Roger's surprised Dr. Abel's so cool about it, but he shouldn't be. Doctors probably deal with this stuff every day. "Yeah. I am."

"Good. How's El Profeto doing?"

The name El Profeto hits Roger like a dump truck. He'd been completely immersed in his LA life, sedated by his blossoming sexuality and José's wealth, but now the full weight of his past comes crashing down.

"He's—I just call him José now, but yeah, he's good."

"That's good. Any plans on coming back?"

"Well, I don't know, we're still playing it safe—"

"The pyramid's shut down, you know."

"What? By who, that guy? 'Cause if it was him you better read that letter—"

"By the county."

"The county? I built that thing in line with every damn building code out there."

"Gachu county."

"What? I haven't heard of any Gachu county in my life!"

"They put a little mini county in the middle of our big one and now the whole town's in Gachu, including the pyramid, and that thing violates just about every code in Gachu's brand new books."

"Then why don't we just vote our people in and get rid of them?"

"That's the thing. The county seat is in a town called Needforasec. Popped up overnight. All those goons moved out there and now they run the show. They outnumber us three to one, what can we do?"

Away from the receiver, Roger groans and presses his forehead to the glass. "Great. Just great. How's the town doing?"

"Bad. Everyone had all their money tied up in the pyramid and damn near every building in town is also in violation. Nobody can run their business. Can you get El Profeto to do something? Maybe buy everyone out so we can pack up and move?"

"Is there really no way you can fight this?"

"Hey, El Profeto's the one who knows fancy lawyers, not me. Just talk to him, alright?"

"Of course. I'm sure he'll figure it out."

"Really?"

"Yeah really, what do you mean?"

"Forget it. Let me know what he says."

"Okay."

"Good to hear from you, Roger."

"You too, Dr. Abel."

"Alright now. Let me know." Dr. Abel hangs up.

When Roger gets back to the apartment, José's awake, boiling some water in the kettle.

"Hey, I was wondering where you went."

"Well I'm back now." Roger shuts the door and takes his shoes off, then slumps down on the couch and turns on the TV. The news is on. It's bad.

"Jeez, what's with the attitude?"

"What attitude? I just went for a walk, now I'm watching TV."

"Yeah, but you're being like, gruff about it." José puts a teabag in his mug.

Roger turns the TV off. "Those goons, the pyramid— the whole town's gone bankrupt!"

"What?"

"I just got off the phone with Dr. Abel." He explains the situation with Gachu county and the new zoning laws. The water finishes boiling and José pours it.

188

"Well that's just crazy. I mean it's totally in character, but I had no idea that guy had so much power he could whip up a new county just to fuck with me."

"And everyone else in town."

"I guess so, but those buildings were falling apart. Maybe it's for the best."

"What, you think everyone can just upgrade their buildings whenever they want just to keep up with the times? Those buildings were all working fine! Well, some of them. But these are your people, your flock! This attack was aimed at you, but it hurt everyone! Aren't you going to help them out?"

"Hey, I can't control every single thing that happens. Some storm blows through town chasing after me, am I supposed to pay for all the downed telephone lines? Like, where in the Pible does it say I have to bail out other people's bad investments?"

"All over the place! Cheesus said a whole bunch of stuff about helping the meek!"

"Those people aren't meek, they're business owners! Things happen in business, they'll figure it out. This can't be their first run of bad luck."

"No, but it's their first run caused by you."

"By me? Are you serious? Whose trunk did I have to hide in with cracked ribs to skip town because of those goons, because of their aggression?"

"They were aggressive because you broke the Sixth Commandment!"

"I broke it because God told me to! And besides, they're breaking a whole bunch of the others too, so they're still worse."

"Like which?"

"A bunch!"

"Be specific!"

"Fuck you, go read the Pible yourself!" José chugs his tea in one scorching gulp and storms off into the bedroom. Roger follows him, spins him around, and holds him up against the wall by his neck.

"Those people believed in you, they trusted you, they gave you everything, and you just walk away like it's not your problem? Fuck you! Without those people, you'd be nothing! Your business would never have gotten off the ground and you would never have been El Profeto, just another crazy weirdo obsessed with the Pible, living upstairs while his wife runs the store and does everything for him! Goddamnit, José, I don't know why I ever believed in you!" He lets go and José falls to the ground, gasping for air and crawling away. Roger follows him back into the living room. José grabs onto the couch and heaves himself up, then picks up his bonsai tree and slips on some sandals.

"Where are you going?"

José opens the door and leaves.

"José!" Roger chases after him out into the hall. José scampers down the stairs and runs outside. He makes it to Roger's car, gets in, and locks the doors just as Roger catches up with him.

"José! Don't do this!"

José buckles up the bonsai in the passenger seat and starts the engine.

Roger bangs on the hood. "That's my car! I'll call the police! I'll tell them you stole it!"

José rolls his window down a crack. "And I'll tell them you strangled me and I had no choice and they'll just laugh it off as a couple of fags having a fag fight! Move!" He honks the horn, but Roger keeps shouting and banging on the hood. He backs up into the car behind him, then swerves out into the road and almost gets t-boned. The

190

other driver lays on the horn, but José speeds off, tires squealing.

Roger's left standing in the street. His face is red and streaked with tears. He goes back inside to get his things and see if José's got any cash stashed away. But even if he could afford a bus ticket, now he can never go home.

20

Laundry, Flowers, Pho. Past New Ribbon. Engine humming. Light in the ocean, shadows on the beach. Relaxing his hands on the wheel. Green light. Left, right, driving down an alley, parking in the back of the Fighting Mambos Precinct #5.

José gets out and digs through his wallet. Wedged behind a bunch of used gift cards and expired memberships, his Fighting Mambos ID is still in there, covered in dust and lint. He swipes it in the scanner by the door. The light turns green and the lock clicks open. He can't believe it still works.

All the lights are off inside. Fumbling around, he finds a switch, but only a couple of the fluorescent tubes buzz to life. What happened here? The place seems completely abandoned. As he walks farther inside, he starts to lose hope until he sees dim light leaking under the door to the library. It creaks as he opens it. Clyde's reading in a leather armchair next to an antique lamp and a coffee table with a bowl of dark green chips and a glass of water on it. He looks up from his book, *Poetry and Combat: The Artistic Nature of Revolution* by Chairman Zao Madong, and smiles for the first time in weeks.

"Well, well, well. If it isn't José Jones."

"What's up, Clyde."

"Take a seat, man. I got some kale chips if you want any."

"Thanks," says José, sitting down across from him. He takes a chip and crunches down. It's horrible.

"Pretty intense, huh?"

192

"Yeah, I don't know if these are really my thing."

"Well that's okay. But you're missing out. The experts say kale's a superfood, so like it or not, us kale eaters are gonna have an edge in life." He scarfs down five of them in one go.

José tries another but that's it. He'll have to find another way to keep up with the kale eaters of the world.

"Been a long time since you came by."

"It has. I was surprised my card still worked."

"Of course, brother." Clyde's sweating bullets. He can't believe he forgot to revoke José's membership.

"But you kicked me out."

"That was a test."

"What?"

"Yeah, man. A loyalty test. You see, after what you did at that factory, you could have become one of our top guys. But before all that, you lied to us about being a CEO."

"I didn't lie!"

"Come on, José. You know the way we roll. If you didn't tell us something big like that, how was I supposed to know how many other secrets you were keeping?"

"I see your point."

Clyde chews a kale chip and just looks at him.

"I guess I failed the test, then."

"Tough to say. If you'd come back here demanding I give you another chance, that might have been an obvious ploy to reinfiltrate our organization on behalf of the powers that be. On the other hand, you might have been truly committed to the cause. And on the flipside, when you didn't come back, it probably meant you knew the jig was up and there was no shot at fooling us again. Or, again, you might have been a loyal soldier for the cause, and if that meant following orders to turn your back on the Fighting Mambos, so be it."

"Then what does any of that prove?"

Clyde shakes his head. "This kind of test ain't a fucking scantron, you feel me? A rat and a true revolutionary could give the exact same answer in the exact same way. But I knew that if you were truly committed, I'd feel your heart through all the bullshit. I'd have been able to sus you out."

José nods. He's a poet, he gets it. "So what's my heart telling you?"

"Well, the test is way over. Doesn't matter now. But you're alright, José. I wish there could have been a way to keep you around back then. Maybe things would have turned out different."

José takes it in, thinks it over. "Thanks, Clyde. That means a lot."

"Tch. Means more to me, if you can believe it. Look at this place, I'm pretty much the only one who hangs out here anymore! Sure, a lot of that's 'cause of the feds. Lot of fake Mambos, lot of setups over the years. We've lost a lot of battles since you've been gone, plenty of comrades sitting in jail these days while everyone else is out there chasing money and all sorts of nonsense. So I appreciate your visit. Especially after that whole siege debacle."

"What siege?"

"You didn't hear?"

"You don't mean..."

"Yeah, that one. We got hoodwinked by that motherfucking Prince of Danger. Thought we were taking over your old company for The People, put our lives on the line to spark a worldwide revolution. But when the dust settled, half our fighters were arrested and the other half scattered to the wind, and all we did was replace your old buddy with some fat cat's stooge."

"Holy—Clyde, I could have told you Michael was no good!"

"I know, Goddamnit!" Clyde slams the table and kale chips fly into the air. "I should have paid you a visit, I should have come up with a different fucking test! Now I'm working dead end fucking jobs to pay the rent on this place so I can chill in here and study theory! Fuck, man!" Clyde throws his book on the ground.

José doesn't know what to say.

Clyde looks up at the portrait of Chairman Zao on the wall and laughs, shakes his head. "I should have listened to Chairman Zao."

"What do you mean?"

"You know, his famous quote."

"Power grows out of the barrel of a gun?"

"Nah, not that one."

"Politics is war by other means."

"Nope. Come on, José, you know the one."

José racks his brain. "Only through the dialectic of revolution shall the contradictions of bourgeois society reach—"

"No! No! No! Why would it be that one?"

"I don't know, it was just a guess."

Clyde sighs. "Alright, well he did say all that stuff. But he also said Friendship is worth more than all treasure under Heaven. You feel me?"

"I think so."

Clyde takes a thoughtful bite of a kale chip, chews it slowly, stares at the portrait. "You came here for a reason, right?"

José nods. "I need your help with something."

"Well alright then." Clyde leans back in his chair and cracks his knuckles. "Lay it on me."

An hour later, José cruises up Mulholland Drive for the last time. He parks Roger's car way off the side of the road behind some bushes, out of sight from any curious cops.

"I'll be back for you, I promise," he says to his bonsai, then gets out and hops the fence of Leon's neighbor's house. He stays low and runs through the side yard, then finds the gap in the hedges and ducks into Leon's garden. Dashing from sculpture to sculpture, he zig-zags his way to the manor. The lights on the ground floor are all out. He lets himself in through the back door, takes his shoes off, and puts them in his coat pockets. The place is eerily silent, but the same as he left it. He sneaks through the dining room, past the couches and the enormous television and down the hall. All his senses are pumping data as fast as he can handle, his life depends on it. He reaches the main hall without a hitch and pokes his head around the corner. No one's coming. He slides across the tiles and climbs the stairs. He hears faint voices. There's a light on in the distance. The den. He tiptoes down the hall until he's right outside the door. Leon and Pete are discussing what sounds like a sequel to *Popcorn Legacy*.

"He's in the popcorn factory, but then he realizes, he is the factory, he's always been the factory, the factory is nothing without him!"

"So then what?"

"He turns his back on popcorn and it all goes up in smoke. Without his genius lubricating the gears, there's nothing to keep the machine humming along!"

"I don't understand. If the workers already know how to make popcorn, why would things shut down just because he left?"

"I mean sure, maybe in real life it wouldn't work that way, but it's a metaphor! Without geniuses, without artists, without poets, hell, without me, myself, I, Pete the Poet!

196

Without my vision, my insights, my teachings, this world would be fucked!"

Leon laughs. "Well now, that's a bit megalomaniacal, don't you think? But still, I'm intrigued by—" He freezes.

"Intrigued by what?"

He nods over at the door. Pete turns around. José's standing in the entrance, a handgun trained on both of them.

"Good evening, José! Long time no see," says Leon, chuckling nervously.

Pete grins. "There you are. I was wondering when you'd show up."

"You were?"

"Sure. With my newfound success in poetry, movies, and romance, all with your former lover, it was only a matter of time."

"What, you think I'm jealous? Just from the poster I could tell your movie's a pile of crap."

"Take that back!"

"And I don't know what Leon told you, but we were never lovers. Far from it."

"What?" Pete glares at Leon, but Leon waves it off.

"If we weren't lovers," asks Leon, "then why are you here pointing a gun at me?"

"Because you drugged me and tried to rape me. Because you've raped dozens of other guys over the years, and they deserve vengeance."

"Don't be ridiculous, José—"

"Get it out."

"What?"

"Your photo album. The one with everyone in it. It's in that drawer over there."

Leon is not amused.

"Go on!" shouts José, waving the gun.

Leon opens the drawer and takes the album out.

"Open it!"

Leon opens it.

"Now start turning the pages, slowly. I want you to look at every last one of them before you die."

He starts flipping through the album. Tears fall on every photo.

Pete's eyes grow wide. "So it's true?"

"It's not," cries Leon. "Don't listen to him, it's not true in the slightest!"

But Leon's not fooling anyone. As he nears the final page, José puts his finger on the trigger, then feels a hand on his shoulder. Smedley's standing behind him, a Tommy gun over his shoulder.

"Relax," he says, and lowers José's arm. Then he gently pushes José aside and trains his gun on Pete and Leon.

"Smedley! What are you doing? Kill him!" shouts Leon.

Smedley shakes his head. "I've enabled you for far too long." He turns to José. "I'm sorry you felt compelled to come out here again. I'm sorry I stood by and said nothing while you were a guest. I'm sorry for all the countless others I let..." Smedley starts crying, but his aim doesn't waver. "My whole life I've been a butler. My father was a butler, his father was a butler. It's the only way of life I know. But it's a way of life for which I must atone. Until now, I've abided by every tenet of the butler's code, no matter the cost. But no longer! I'm more than just a butler! I'm a human being! I'm done standing by and watching as you ruin people's lives!"

"No, Smedley, please, wait, I'll give you a raise—"

But Smedley screams and blasts away at them, sending five shots through Leon's chest, one through Pete's head, and a dozen others through the bookshelf and chaise-longue, paper and feathers flying everywhere, drifting down, settling afloat the pooling blood. He lowers his gun and keeps sobbing.

José's shaking. "You… you killed Pete too!"

Smedley nods.

"But why?"

"That guy had issues, José, serious issues. He was only with Leon to make you jealous."

"Yeah I knew that, but that doesn't mean he deserved—"

"Then you didn't know. Not the full story. Look, I'm going to call the police in a minute and turn myself in, so you should get out of here. But trust me. Pete was going to be the next Fütler if I let him keep going."

"Really? But he's just an artist, I don't really know if he was planning on getting into politics—"

"So was Fütler when he was young, and now the rest is history. I've seen a lot around here, okay? The deed is done. Can you just trust me on this?"

José really wants a better explanation, but he nods.

"Thank you. Seriously. Now go!"

José dashes out and slips and falls in the hallway, then takes his shoes out of his pockets, puts them on, and runs downstairs.

When he gets in Roger's car, he can already hear the sirens. He starts it up and drives off, passing three police cruisers on his way down the hill. Now what? He's not actually a murderer, not this time anyways, so is Clyde's escape plan even necessary anymore? He glances over at the bonsai, hoping for an answer. But the bonsai says nothing, and by saying nothing, tells him he can figure it out for himself. And he does. It's easy. Just look at his life. The Important Client is still after him so he has to wear a disguise everywhere, Roger hates him, that town's probably gonna sue him for millions of dollars, and just because Smedley's the one who shot Pete and Leon doesn't mean José's off the hook if any cameras caught him breaking in. The more he thinks about life in LA, the more he just wants to leave it all behind.

He pulls up at the docks and parks Roger's car. Clyde's waiting for him at the spot. He unbuckles the bonsai and walks over to him. They shake hands and bring it on in, then José hands him his gun.

"It's over," he says.

"Whoa, I told you to throw that thing out," says Clyde.

"Sorry, I forgot."

Clyde sighs. "It's cool, bro. I'll take care of it." He slides the gun down his waistband. José feels bad for letting Clyde think it's a murder weapon because guns aren't cheap, but this is the first action Clyde's seen in years and José doesn't want to let him down.

"You ready?" asks Clyde.

"Yes, sir."

"Then let's get it." They walk past the gates and up the gangplank to an enormous container ship. Clyde fistbumps the guard and they weave through the containers until they reach the one with a chalk X drawn on it, right by the side of the boat. Clyde rubs it off, then opens the door. It's cramped, but the container is outfitted with a bed, a desk, a lamp, a five-hundred gallon water tank, boxes of dried foodstuffs, and a stack of revolutionary literature, history, and theory.

"Wasn't easy putting this together," says Clyde. "But my man came through."

"This is perfect," says José. "But... sorry, how do I use the bathroom?"

Clyde laughs. "There's a bucket in there, and there's a circle in the side of the container that unscrews so you can dump it all overboard."

"Got it."

"And here." Clyde hands him a bottle of tequila. José turns it over and sees a smiling cactus wearing a sombrero, waving its maracas in a festive setting on the label. A part of him wants to hand it back, but he doesn't.

"That's your brand, right?"

José nods. "Si. Thanks."

"Of course."

There's a long pause.

"Well alright then. You ready?"

"I guess so."

Clyde gives him a hug, then José goes inside. "Stay strong, comrade. You know I'll still be holding it down for the revolution over here."

"I know you will, man. Thanks for everything."

"No, José. Thank you." Clyde salutes him, then closes the door. He nods to the guard before he walks down the gangplank, then the ship blows its horn. As he watches it sail off into the Pacific, away to distant lands, his eyes fill with tears, and he lets himself cry for the first time in a long time.

21

Forty years later, Sino-American tensions are at an all-time high. Between average citizens and top government officials, the media and the fake media, the left and the right, everyone agrees that unless something's done to turn things around, it's gonna be bad. President Carlos Buenavista has just been elected on the promise of restoring hope and averting catastrophe, a promise he intends to keep. Under cover of darkness, he and Secretary of State Leroy McMenahan fly out to Beijing in a secret last-ditch effort to broker peace. Their arrival is muted. There's no welcoming committee, no fanfare, just a delegation in suits waiting on the tarmac. The President and his team are escorted into bulletproof limousines and driven to the secret location. Rubbing his eyes and massaging his temples, President Buenavista tries to wake up and clear his head.

"Sleep well?" asks Secretary of State McMenahan.

"Well as I could."

"Lucky."

"What, you didn't sleep?"

Secretary of State McMenahan shakes his head. "I can never sleep on planes."

"Yeah, that turbulence was something," says President Buenavista, gazing out the window at the Chinese cityscape.

After forty-five minutes, they arrive at a nondescript office building. They're escorted inside, up the elevator, and down the hall to a secure room that's been vetted by both American and Chinese personnel to be free of recording devices, internet and cellphone reception, and anything else that might interfere with the negotiations. They enter and bow to President Zhou Huasei and his associates, and the Chinese in turn stand and bow. The parties sit. President Zhou smiles.

"Thank you for taking the time to fly all the way to Beijing. I hope your travels were uneventful." His American is impeccable.

"They were, President Zhou," says President Buenavista. "Thank you for hosting us in your beautiful country."

President Zhou gives a slight, respectful nod. "Please, we are in private company. Call me Huasei."

"If you don't mind, President Zhou, I'd like to stick to our official titles today. This is a serious situation, and it would not do to forget the gravity of our circumstances for even a moment."

"As you wish." President Zhou cracks his knuckles. "Now, where shall we begin?"

Secretary of State McMenahan shuffles through some papers he's brought and finds the one he wants. "Well to start, President Zhou, I think we need to figure out a way to de-escalate the situation in the South China Sea. No more skirmishes."

"But Secretary of State McMenahan, it is my understanding that the United States has initiated every one of the recent skirmishes. China is only acting in self-defense."

Secretary of State McMenahan frowns. If they can't even agree on the basic facts, how are they going to get anything done?

Hours go by and hope for a peaceful resolution fades. They can't agree on who started what, when, and why, and the concessions each side offers just won't cut it. Finally, President Zhou stands up.

"I think that's enough for today. You are both still tired from your journey. I commend you for getting right to business after such a long flight. Please, get some rest, and we will continue our discussion in the morning."

President Buenavista and Secretary of State McMenahan are still brimming with arguments, but President Zhou's right. They need sleep.

The next day, things aren't much better. The discussions are more lucid and eloquent, but the two sides are still locked in a stalemate. Right as things reach a boiling point, when President Buenavista and Secretary of State McMenahan can barely restrain themselves from leaping across the table and giving this smug jerk what's coming to him, President Zhou asks that everyone leave the room, everyone but the American President and Secretary of State. President Buenavista nods to the secret service, and they and their Chinese counterparts file out. Now it's just the three of them. President Zhou leans back in his chair and kicks his feet up on the table.

"You still don't see it, huh?"

"See what?" asks President Buenavista, but President Zhou only smiles. Leroy finally notices the intricate bonsai tree in the corner of the room.

"It can't be…"

President Zhou laughs through his nose. "Oh, but it can. I could never fool you, Leroy."

"But—but how?"

"What's going on?" asks President Buenavista.

"You tell him," says President Zhou.

"President Buenavista. This… is our old friend, José Jones."

President Buenavista squints at the Chinese leader and sees it in his eyes. "Holy shit."

"My face has changed a lot since I got here," says President Zhou. "One of the first things I shelled out for was surgery. I needed a new look for my new life, and oh how it paid off!"

"But you're an American!" cries President Buenavista.

"Not anymore! For forty years now I've been a Chinese citizen. In this country, anything can be bought if you have enough money and know the right people, and China has been most kind to me!"

"Has it?" asks Secretary of State McMenahan, his patriotic arms folded.

President Zhou smiles but his lips quiver and his face twitches like a malfunctioning robot, and suddenly it all comes pouring out, the trauma, the repression, the denial.

"No! It hasn't!" President Zhou sprawls on the table, sobbing his heart out. President Buenavista offers him a tissue, but even if President Zhou accepted it'd be like trying to clean up an oil spill with a mop. "You don't know the things I've had to do! The people I've betrayed, the lives I've ruined, the crimes I've committed! Crimes against God, crimes against my soul!" José throws his hands up and addresses heaven. "Oh, why did I come here? Why did I do it all?"

No one can answer that for him.

"Well it was all worth it in the end, right?" asks President Buenavista. "I mean, look at you! You're President Zhou! Who would have thought—"

"It wasn't! It wasn't!" He cries and cries and cries. "I miss Mama! I miss Papa! I miss Jorge! I wish I was a kid again! Why can't we all get along and be nice to each other? Why does being a grown up have to be so horrible?!" He collapses into deeper sorrow and a pool of tears spreads across the negotiating table.

President Buenavista and Secretary of State McMenahan go over to him. They sit down on each side and rub his back.

"It's gonna be okay, José," says Leroy, tears in his eyes. "We're gonna work this out.

I promise.